TEMPTING THE HEIRESS

NANA MALONE

COPYRIGHT

Tempting the Heiress, Book e in the Heiress Duet

Cover Art by Hang Le

Photography by Wander Aguilar

Edited by Angie Ramey and Michele Ficht

Published in the United States of America

To all my fellow nerds, thank you for always seeing me.

ONE

JAX...

She knew...

The one thing I hadn't been able to tell her. The one lie I'd told.

It was a pretty big lie.

I knew how betrayed she'd felt by fuckface. I knew, but I'd still lied.

For the job.

I never should have touched her.

There was no making her listen. She handed me my magazine and whirled to hoof it back in the house.

I had to make a decision; Attempt to stop her or continue.

Shit.

Ariel needed to know. Just how much did I tell her? And how much would she be able to figure out on her own?

I climbed back in the driver's seat, my heart hammering.

Talk about fucking things up.

My conscience was having a field day. I'd known how this would end, and I'd still fucked up in all manner of places. I hadn't been able to keep my hands off of her. I hadn't closed my damn door or made sure shit was locked up tight.

I'd been in a hurry this morning. Mayzie had been impatient.

You spent half your prep time eating pussy.

Fuck. Yeah, that too. There was no excuse for this morning other than I wanted to make her hum. It had been a deliberate choice, and now she was walking away.

If I'd have just closed the drawer or brought the damn toy downstairs... I must have left it in my room on my way to get Mayzie for some reason.

Or your brain was too addled from boning the client.

Shit.

It would be useless going after her, so I made my choice. Let her go. I'd fucked up. It was time to right the goal train. My goal was to get back in the Guard. I needed to try to make that happen. It didn't matter how much my heart squeezed. Chasing after Neela was only going to hurt her more. As I drove past the security gate, I called Ariel.

"I see you, Jax. I'll wait five minutes and then go up."

"We have a problem."

Ariel's voice went tense, alert. "What?"

"She knows."

There was a beat of silence. "What?" It sounded more like an expletive.

"Yeah, she found one of my gun magazines in my room."

"Holy shit."

"I know. She's pretty pissed off. But she didn't stop me from taking Mayzie."

“What the ever-loving fuck? Did you say something dumb, do something dumb before she found it?"

If you mean did I bone her senseless and give her enough orgasms to make her actually physically pass out, then yes.

I skirted the truth. "She feels betrayed, Ariel. We both know she didn't want security."

"Son of a bitch."

"That's basically what I said with more colorful language. We should have told her."

"Now is not the time."

"I know. But it might have been easier. Now she feels betrayed. I don't know if she's going to let you in."

"Shit. I'm on my way in. Let's fucking hope I'm able to talk her down."

"If you think you can. Either way, she might not let *me* back in the house."

"Well, she let you leave with the baby, so that can only be a good sign."

"I know, but still. She probably wasn't even thinking about Mayzie at the time."

"Maybe, maybe not. I'll test it out. Okay, stay on plan. Go to the park as usual. I'll go see her."

"Roger that."

"I'll find a way to fix it. I always do." She hung up before I had a chance to ask any more questions.

I glanced into the back seat. "Mayzie, what are we going to do with your mom?"

Mayzie, cute as she was, unhelpfully blew me a raspberry. After all, she wasn't the one who screwed up. I was. And right about now, I needed a miracle to fix it.

ARIEL...

This was the last thing I wanted to deal with. This was fucked on an epic scale. Now I had to deal with a pissed-off client who wasn't even our actual client.

Jax was right, we should have told her. But technically Bipps was the client, not her. So, we were doing exactly as we were told, but she might start to make our jobs a lot more difficult.

I drove up to the security gate, ready to force my way in there if I had to. But I was allowed in, no problem.

I parked the car and jogged up the stairs to the house. When I knocked, no one came for a moment. Was she deliberately not answering? Would I have to break into the place I was meant to protect?

It had been a while since I'd picked a lock, but I could manage it if I had to.

Or, you can relax. She might be in the back.

When Neela finally opened the door, she glowered at me. "You know, I should have trusted my instincts. No way in hell were you guys nannies."

"Your instincts probably told you exactly what we are, but people believe what they need to. I'm so sorry you were caught up in this."

"Who the hell are you people? I trusted you. I trusted him... with my child."

"Look, let's take this conversation inside."

"No. We will not take this conversation inside. We will have this conversation right the hell here."

I shuffled on my feet. Fantastic. Just freaking fantastic. I could remind her that she wasn't actually in charge here, but it would be better for my man inside and for everybody else if I could diffuse the situation.

"Okay, I get it. You're pissed off. You *should* be pissed off. We lied to you. There's no other way around that. But know that we were doing it to protect you. And most importantly, to protect Mayzie.

"How? By keeping me in the dark? I had a man watching my baby who had no business watching a baby."

I leveled my gaze on her. "Are you saying Jax wasn't good with Mayzie?"

She frowned, deep furrows forming on her brow. "That's not what I'm saying. But he's hardly *qualified*."

Ah, so this was a Jax problem. She was pissed he'd lied to her. I watched her closely. That wasn't anger I was seeing. It was hurt. Fabulous. She'd decided she liked the guy, which could work for us or really, *really* work against us.

"He's better qualified than anyone else. He has medic training and hordes of nieces and nephews he helped raise. You've seen him with her yourself. He actually loves that little girl."

"Oh yeah, and he's carrying a gun around her, for what?" she sputtered.

"Listen. I know this is a shock, but Mr. Bipps was quite insistent that you have security."

At the mention of Bipps, she crossed her arms. "Here's the thing you don't realize; Mayzie's *mine* now. *My* responsibility. It's *my* right to choose how she gets raised. Mr. Bipps had no right to call you."

I was about to burst that bubble. "Be that as it may, he still called us. He's the executor. You're the guardian. You handle the day to day, but he is in charge of the big picture. He believes she's in danger. And given the note you received and the attempted kidnapping, don't you see that you need us?"

She glowered at me. "I guess I shouldn't be surprised that you know about the note."

"Of course not. Jax works for me."

Her brow lifted then. As though she hadn't expected that. "Whatever arrangement you guys have, I don't care. I don't care who works for whom or who was following whose orders. I do not care. You people lied to me."

"And I get that. You're pissed off, and you should be. For what it's worth, Jax was begging to tell you the truth. The orders were not to."

She narrowed her gaze at me as if trying to ascertain the truth of my statement. "That does not make any of this better."

"I didn't imagine it would. But it's still the truth."

"For weeks. You guys have been here for *weeks*."

"And we've been hunting down leads. At least now that you know you can help us. Because, we're here for Mayzie. But we're also here for you. To protect you."

She shook her head. "How is this my life?"

"I wish I knew. I wish the most important thing to you was where to party tonight. I wish your life could be all Mommy and Me and baby yoga or whatever. But it can't be. Not right now. As soon as we find out who's targeting you, you can have your life back. You'll never have to see us again."

"I'm going to hold you to that."

For a long tense moment, we stood at stand-off positions; her in the doorway, me trying to figure out the best way past her without hurting her. But as it turned out, none of that was necessary. She stepped aside and let me in. Now all I had to do was hope she'd do the same for Jax.

"I know you're angry. You can call Mr. Bipps. He did hire us."

She frowned. "But I researched you. The testimonials. The reviews."

Oh boy. "All faked. I'm pretty good with a computer."

"Jesus Christ. You weren't even real. Is *any* of this real?"

"Yes. How Jax feels about that baby is real. And he is damn good with her, you have to admit that. He's here to protect the both of you."

She scowled then and muttered under her breath, "Yeah, but who's going to protect me from him?"

TWO

NEELA...

I WAS DONE. Tired and done, and I'd had bloody enough.

My whole life since my father died, people had made decisions for me, and never in my best interest. I wasn't going to let that happen anymore.

Oh yeah? What are you going to do about it?

I scowled into my rearview mirror. I could see the SUV following me. It only made me more determined. I knew who they worked for, so I was going straight to the source.

Jax still had Mayzie out, which was fine. As angry as I was at him, Ariel was right. He was good with Mayzie. And, as he was a bodyguard, he would make sure nothing happened to her. But why couldn't anyone see that the things *I* worried about were along the lines of was she healthy, was she eating enough, and not, is someone going to shoot her? I didn't run some drug cartel. I ran a small business. No one cared about me.

Or maybe Ariel is right, and this isn't about you at all. Maybe it's about Mayzie.

If that was the truth, then we really were screwed. Who the hell in their right mind would come after a baby?

I kept thinking back to my initial conversation with Mr. Bipps. He insinuated that there were people who would want to kidnap that little girl.

Which to me had seemed ridiculous. But it was a distinct possibility. I couldn't ignore that anymore. Someone had tried to grab me off the street.

Maybe it wasn't about you at all. Maybe it was about Mayzie.

If that was the case, what was the note about?

The only person who could give me answers was about a half mile ahead. And he was going to give me some damn answers if it killed him.

I swung the car into a parking spot haphazardly, not caring that the car took up the only two spots available. Whoever the hell Ariel had in the SUV, they could find somewhere else to park and walk.

Maybe I was being a little childish, but I was done. I'd run out of fucks to give, and I was taking no prisoners. I yanked the heavy glass door open and marched in, startling the receptionist. "Ms. Wellbrook, Mr. Bipps isn't expecting—"

I didn't let her finish. I just kept marching right past her and barged right into Bipps's office. The poor man was trying to eat a sandwich, but screw that. He'd ruined my day, so the very least I could do was damn well ruin his lunch.

"Ms. Wellbrook, I didn't expect you."

"A security team?"

He was mid-stand as he was coming around to greet me, but I was pretty sure the vibe I was putting off was, 'Sit your ass down.'

He did sit. "How did you find out?"

"That's not the point. The point is I was very clear and

specific, I did not *want* security. You might act old and doddering, but I get the impression you're quite sharp, so I know you must have heard me."

"I did hear you." He steepled his fingers and sat back. "I also know that you were naive in your request."

"Naive? What the hell is wrong with you people? My whole life, Willa, her parents, asshole Dick, and now you have attempted to tell me what I should be doing, how I should be doing it... One day, one of you assholes is going to have to let me live my life."

He inhaled a long breath and released it. "Ms. Wellbrook, Neela, I'm sorry that this was necessary. But I believe that there is a clear and present danger toward Mayzie and perhaps even yourself."

"You control her money and what would be best for her finances, but you do not control *me*."

He sighed. "You're correct. I do not control you. But as executor of Willa's estate, I do control where that money gets spent. Which covers housing, child care, schooling for Mayzie..."

"You're going to wield that like a weapon, aren't you? Newsflash, I've dealt with worse. Jane MacKenzie was the worst of the worst. She knew how to wield manipulation like a finely-honed weapon. You are an amateur compared to her."

He sighed again. "Ms. Wellbrook, I'm not trying to wield any weapons. I'm trying to keep that baby safe and to keep you safe by extension."

"By sticking an *armed* guard on her?"

"I'm sorry that had to happen, and I'm sorry that it was done without your consent. But it was necessary."

"Who exactly do you think is after her?"

"It could be anyone. As we discussed, Miss MacKenzie didn't make the best associations."

"She's dead. You can tell me. I can call the police."

His dark, narrowed gaze pinned me to my seat. "And tell them what exactly?" He sat back again. "Have you been through her financial records yet?"

"Yes. They are pristine."

"Yes, they do *appear* pristine. Who do you know that runs a small business that has the cleanest books ever? You run a small business. I know for a fact that your business is on the up-and-up. How pristine are your books?"

I shifted in my seat. "There's always at least an invoice missing. There's always someone who hasn't paid. There's always something that's a little off."

He nodded. "Exactly. I'm sure by now you have noticed there is some missing inventory."

I frowned, my gut knotting tighter. "Yes, there have been some calls."

He gave me a sharp nod. "I don't know exactly what Willa was into, but I know that for a young woman who dealt mostly in avant-garde art, she had a lot of revenue coming in. A revenue she was happy to pay taxes on. But there is also revenue that I might not even be tracing for her. She would buy property in cash. She traveled a lot extensively to other places in the islands. I know the Cayman's were her favorite. I know she likes to go to Switzerland."

"You're saying Willa was laundering money?"

"Amongst other things. It's not how I run a business. But with the sheer amount of money she was bringing in, I had to ask questions. And when I did, she stopped bringing me that kind of business. No more real estate deals in her daughter's name. I think she maybe has another lawyer somewhere. But she did let me handle things about the estate, and everything is in Mayzie's name. When I say everything is in Mayzie's name, I'm not kidding. *Everything* is in Mayzie's name. From the house to the cars. That kid has more things on her credit report than you do. Luckily, she's never defaulted. And she's probably not even out of diapers."

The breath came whooshing out of my chest. "Oh my God, Willa, what have you done?"

Mr. Bipps nodded slowly. "I'm sorry. I know that you probably feel like I forced this on you."

"You *did* force this on me. I don't want this. I don't want these people following me around. I certainly don't want guns around Mayzie."

"I understand. But I can't let Mayzie go unprotected. I assume you found out because someone told you?"

"No, I found a gun magazine."

His brow furrowed. "I heard Ms. Scott and her people were the best. Did they make a mistake?"

This was the place, the crossroads, the place where I could choose to toss Ariel and her team under the bus or let them run their little business. I had the power to do that, and even though there was an evil part of me that wanted to do it, there was no way I could. I knew how hard it was running a business. I knew how hard it was making things work. "I was snooping. They never seemed like nannies to me. That's how I found the magazine."

"Well then, it seems I underestimated you."

"Yeah, you can say that again."

"Look, I'll make you a deal. As soon as we find out how

serious the threat is against Mayzie or you, then you can have your life back. Any decisions after that would be made between the two of us for Mayzie."

I narrowed my gaze at him. "This is my I-know-better face."

"Well, you will just have to trust me."

"Unfortunately, I've learned not to trust a damn soul. I need to look after myself."

"Maybe, but maybe you'll see that this team is exactly what you need."

Neela...

I WISH I could say I felt better after the conversation with Bipps, but I didn't. At the end of the day, I still felt powerless. Completely manipulated with zero options. But they all made a mistake underestimating me. I didn't just have to take it. I didn't just have to accept what was happening. My whole life had been accepting what was happening to me.

No more.

Back at the house, I marched straight through the door. I ignored Jax, who was back with Mayzie and feeding her lunch. He started to speak, and I just shook my head at him. I stooped to give Mayzie a kiss, and she gave me a sweet drooly one in return.

I'd only had her a few short weeks, but I would do anything to protect her now. She was mine. And protecting her meant getting these yahoos out of our house. To do that, I needed my team.

I headed out the back door. Jax called after me, but I ignored him.

Once I was in the guest house, Bex and Adam both looked up. Bex always took an earlier lunch and Adam preferred a later one, so I could almost guarantee to find them both at twelve thirty.

Something about the look on my face must have told Adam that something was up. "What's wrong?"

Bex's question was a bit more straightforward. "Who do I kill?"

I sighed. "It's been a long morning. I'm sorry. But basically, those yahoos inside, primarily Jax, are not nannies. They're security."

Adam chuckled. "Well, I could have told you that."

Bex lifted a brow. "Well, I mean, when you said they were nannies, I was like, 'They look like no nannies I've ever seen.' Now that you say they're security, it makes sense. But what are they guarding?"

"That's just the thing. They *say* they're guarding Mayzie. They *say* they're guarding me. But right now, I trust no one."

I glanced over at Bex's desk where she was pulling out various letter openers from the drawers.

"What are you doing?"

"Armoring up."

I rolled my eyes. "Bex, we're not armoring up just yet. We need to fight them in a way I know how to fight."

This excited Adam because he knew exactly what I meant. "We're going to fuck with their taxes and basically put the tax man on their asses for the rest of eternity?"

"Close." Damn, they were vengeful. "We're going to do the

one thing I've been unable to do so far." I pulled the ledger out of my bag and held it up. We're going to crack this. When we crack this, they'll be able to find out who the hell is after me and Mayzie, and then they can get the hell out of my house."

Bex studied me. "Okay. So where are you on it?"

"Besides realizing it's a ledger and not a journal, nowhere."

Adam stuck out his hand. "Give it here."

I handed it over and he quickly thumbed through it. "I assume you have already gone through all the typical language-base searches."

"Yeah. It's the first thing I did. I can't find the common language at all, and it's making me insane."

"Okay, I'll see what I can do with it."

"It's all hands on deck. Bex, you too."

"Hey, I'm a baby with this stuff. You guys are the real geniuses."

"Maybe, but you're great at seeing patterns. It's all of us on this now. I don't want to live in Fort Knox."

Bex leaned closer. "So that guy, Jax, he's like a real-life action hero? For real?"

"Yeah, for real. I mean, look at him. I was an idiot if I ever thought he was a nanny."

Adam snorted. "Well, I mean, the good news is he's there to protect Mayzie, right?"

I nodded. "That's what Bipps says. But Bipps also said that he didn't really know what Willa was up to, but I get the impression that he's in up to his neck. So right now, from this point forward, we only trust the three people in this room. Tweedle Dee out there will get nothing from us." I hitched my thumb toward the house.

Bex and Adam slid each other glances. I didn't care what they thought at that point. I needed to protect myself, Mayzie, and my company.

Jax and his team had fucked with me, which meant they needed to go. I had a zero-assholes policy, and Royal Elite was currently *persona non grata.* But first things first; I had to figure out the ledger.

Adam began to make copies. Bex took my hand and pulled me outside, not toward the courtyard but around the side of the guesthouse by the pool.

"Are you okay?"

"Yep, fine."

"Look, you marched in there and told us those guys are security. That must be affecting you in some way."

"It's fine, Bex. I'm fine. Everything is *fine.*"

"Yeah, because your hair is on fire. And you look... hurt."

"I'm not hurt. It's just that I'm tired of living like this. Waiting for the other shoe to drop. Waiting for the next person in my life to hurt me."

"Well, you have me and Adam. We would never hurt you."

"I know. Just... Willa, her family, Richard, Jax... Honestly, it's enough to give a girl a complex."

"Just because *they* are dickheads it doesn't mean everyone else is, okay? Adam and I, we got you. The three of us, the Three Musketeers, we'll figure out this ledger, and then we'll get everyone out of your hair. Okay?"

I nodded. I could feel the tears pricking behind my lids, but I would not let them fall. Jax Reynolds, if that was even his real name, would not make me cry.

Yeah, sure. I was a complete idiot for falling for those soulful eyes, his hot touches, the heated glances... I'd fallen for that. Believed they were real. Believed that he could care about me.

That was my bad, and I was going to make sure it would never happen again. What's done was done. The sooner I got rid of Royal Elite, the better off we'd all be.

THREE

JAX...

So, this was the game we were playing now.

Neela wasn't talking to me. And I had to pretend that I didn't see her not talking to me. It was ridiculous.

Once I put Mayzie down, I squared my shoulders as I stood outside her room. I knocked gently, but she didn't say anything, didn't come to the door.

And what did you expect, that she'd talk to you?

The thing was, I could hear her moving around in there. She went completely still when I knocked. But after she thought I had walked away, she started moving again. "Neela, I can hear you."

Finally, the footsteps approached the door and she opened it. "What?"

"I just want to—"

She put up a hand and cut me off. "Is this about Mayzie? Is she sick, colicky? Hungry?"

I frowned and shook my head. "No, she's down. She's asleep."

"Then we have nothing to say to each other." She tried to close the door again, but I wedged my foot inside to stop her.

"Look, I know it feels like I betrayed you. Believe me, I wanted to tell you."

"But somehow you managed to *not* do that and still sleep with me."

She has a point there, wanker. "That wasn't supposed to happen. You know that. I tried to—"

"What? You tried to *not* fuck me?"

I winced. "That's what you think it was?"

"What else would it be? It's not like you have any real feelings for me. Or like I have any for you, for that matter. You were just a hot body I happened to use."

I knew it was bullshit, but it still stung. "I know you don't mean that."

"You don't know me at all. Just like I don't know you, apparently."

Direct hit. "Look, all I'm trying to tell you is the stuff with you and me wasn't supposed to happen. But the moment you walked into that office, I knew that staying away from you was going to be impossible. And—" I ran my hands through my hair. "I tried. God knows I tried. Then you sent that text and being with you was all that I could think about. I wanted you so bad I finally broke. There was no staying away from you."

It was her turn to wince. "I would rather not be reminded of my mistakes. Or in this case, Bex's."

"I'm not trying to do that. I'm just trying to... explain, I guess. The mission was to protect Mayzie. Protect you. Say nothing. Maintain the cover. I wasn't supposed to fall for you. It wasn't my intention."

"Was any of it real? Anything you said to me?"

"Everything I said to you was true."

"Except for the part where you told me you were a manny."

"For this mission, I *am* a manny. I just also happen to be a bodyguard."

She glowered at me. "Semantics. You really think you're going to get away with pretending that you did not lie for your own purposes?"

"You think I wanted to lie to you? Do you think I wanted to see that hurt and betrayed look on your face? It's killing me to see it. Knowing I put it there. Knowing I could have stopped it. I begged Ariel to tell you the truth. I thought you could handle it. But you aren't the client."

She winced again. "So I keep being told. Bipps is. And believe me, I would not choose to be the client."

"I understand. I get it. This isn't how you wanted this to happen. Trust me, the last thing I wanted was to tell you this or have you find out this way. And you and I... I didn't plan that. It wasn't supposed to happen. I didn't know it *could* happen. I was pretty much dead inside. And then in you walked, you and that baby. I started to feel things I was never supposed to feel."

She shook her head, put up her hand, and walked away. "I'm done."

I marched in after her. "Fine. You don't have to talk. I'll talk. I told myself I didn't want any ties. I didn't want a family any more. I didn't want any of it. After what happened the last time, I was just finally starting to get my life back on track. Get my shit together. Coming out of the fog of having everything ripped away from me. You weren't expected. I didn't want to fall for you. Everything I've been working for would be in jeopardy if I did."

She wasn't listening. She was folding Mayzie's clothes, completely ignoring me. But I had to continue.

"Your love and generosity, the way you look at Mayzie, the way you stand up for what you think is right, all those things are what drew me to you. You are strong and stubborn and so damn sexy, and I am honored to even be in your presence. That's how I feel about you. I wish I didn't. I wish I could make it go away. I wish it had never happened. But there it is, the truth. And you can do with it what you will."

She still didn't turn around to face me, but I knew she'd heard me. Her shoulders were stiff and tight and bunched up around her ears. Oh, she'd heard me all right.

What she did with it was up to her. But for the first time since meeting her, I'd told her the complete and utter truth.

***Neela*...**

THAT THING they said about things looking better in the morning... that was a lie. Nothing looked better in the morning. I still had a gaping hole where my heart should be. I still was no closer to the answers in the ledger. And I still had a goddamn security detail.

Except, now it was worse. One of the other guards, Jameson, had kitted out the second guest house with surveillance equipment and was also staying there.

And I'd made the mistake of letting Jax speak to me. The low rumble of his voice as he told me everything I'd ever wanted to hear from him, or any man, was a recipe for disaster as I'd tried to sleep. Not only because what he said confused me and I didn't know if I could believe him or not, but also because now that he'd touched me... I was a little addicted.

I needed it. The night before, with him in my doorway smelling like clean spices, I'd almost broken and just kissed him. As it was, I hadn't been able to sleep. I'd tossed and turned until finally, I'd dragged out the one vibrator I had to my name and put it to good use.

Twice.

Only then had I been able to fall into a fitful sleep with dreams of Jax to keep me riding the edge of need. I'd woken up cranky and irritable and was convinced he could tell exactly what I'd been up to last night. With every glance or accidental—or maybe not-so-accidental—brush of his body that morning, I could see the heat flare in his eyes.

Despite what he'd done, I still wanted him.

My brain tried to perform an intervention: *None of it was real.*

Had his plan been to sleep with me all along? To make me more malleable?

Libido: *But it felt real.*

This was what happened when I let my libido drive. This was what happened when I took risks.

My eyes stung, but I refused to cry. I would not cry, for the love of God. I'd messed up, but I sure as hell didn't need to have a pity party. I had work to do.

Bex met me at the door. "There you are. I was going to mount a search—" She stopped abruptly. "Did he say something to upset you?"

Yes. "No. Let's get to work."

I should have known she wouldn't let it go, though. "Honey.

I'll believe nothing is wrong the moment that I believe Richard has a big dick."

I shook my head. "Not today Bex. Just... not today."

She quieted. "Did that fucker do something to you last night?"

In a matter of speaking. "No. And maybe that's the problem. I love you, but I need you to drop it, okay?"

She frowned at me. "Okay, fine. You don't have to talk about it right now. But you can't hold it in. No one expects you to fix everything. You are not supposed to. All you can fix is what you can control."

Adam came in with a wide smile. "Hey, boss lady. I'm still working on the ledger. I have a program trying to work it out."

"Thanks, Adam." I hurried into my office and dropped off my bag before either one of them looked too closely. I grabbed my laptop and then I was back out the door again. "Bex, you're with me at the gallery, right? I want to see if there are any clues in there that will help us figure out that ledger."

Her voice was soft when she answered. "Yeah. I've got a plan for the inventory. Just to make sure we didn't miss anything. Willa was pretty organized with this. I want to see if she's got anything in there that will help me identify who the clients are. She only used numbers and some kind of complex voodoo to ascertain who they are, because deliveries were made, as far as I can tell. But it's hard to tell what's what."

Adam slid me another gaze. "While you two do that and the algorithm is running the ledger, I'm going to handle re-pitching some of the clients that left us to go with Richard. We're almost at one month. We had to let them go, but if they've since fired him, we can woo them back."

Shit. Now I was really going to cry. What the hell had I done to deserve these guys on my team?

"Thank you. Both of you."

Bex squeezed my hand. "You got it. Now let's go to the gallery and see what we're dealing with."

I cleared my throat. "About that. We're going to have some company."

She frowned. "Who?"

"You'll see."

The blond woman, Tamsin, was on duty in the foyer, and she stood as soon as we came out.

"How did you know we were coming out?"

She tapped her phone. "You forget we've got cameras in there?"

I sighed. "That's going to take some getting used to." I turned to glare at Zia. "Let's go."

Bex did not move.

Bex managed to keep her mouth shut about the cameras until we were in the car, but she kept shooting me her wide-eyed, holy-fuck face. When I ignored her, too caught up in my own holy-fuck-I slept-with-a-total-liar spin out, she leaned forward and spoke to Tamsin. "So, let me get this straight. You're just like... a bodyguard." She eyed her up and down. "But you're like... hot."

Tamsin grinned. "Thank you. But just because I'm blonde with perky tits doesn't mean I don't know my way around a gun."

Bex waved a hand. "I know. That's not what I meant, but I don't know. What made you want to, you know, guard bodies? For real though, you guys are like the hot bodyguard agency. I knew there was no way you guys were nannies."

I could see Zia roll her eyes in the rearview mirror from the driver's seat, and it brought a small smile to my face.

Considering my mood, I was amazed I was capable of feeling anything besides fury. Not just at Jax, but at Willa for making any of this necessary.

We were at the gallery in no time. I looked at the gallery, and it was much the same. Zia was in charge of the car, and Tamsin took us inside.

Her head was on a swivel, constantly paying attention. Bex and I went in, and Tamsin took her post. The first place Bex went was straight for the inventory room.

Bex was efficient as hell once she got over the fact that cameras might be everywhere. She was like a little buzzing bee, all over everything. She started at the very tip top and moved her way through, explaining to me which pieces were which, which pieces made no sense, and which ones she couldn't place. There were three or four we couldn't place. Vases and sculptures mostly, and one of them rattled a little inside, making me worried a piece had broken off.

She opened her phone. "I've been trying to track the original artists listed next to each piece. That's another puzzle all together."

"Let me do that, actually. I want to feel useful." I'd brought the journal along to take another crack at it. But I still had no basis for the code, so I was just spinning my wheels.

I dug in, trying to make sense of the current year's sales. At least they should be easier to track down. That part made sense. The numbers, the dates, the organization. Little puzzle pieces falling into place. Not the mish-mash of bullshit that had become my life of late.

A crash in the inventory room had me on my feet. I ran

toward Bex, and she was shaking her head. "Shit. I didn't mean to. I mean, I picked it up and the damn thing just crumbled out of my hands. I swear to God I—"

I held up my hand to stop the stream of consciousness pouring from her mouth. She'd dropped a sculpture. But amongst the debris was something else. I kneeled down in the mess and brushed the big chunks away.

There was a scroll. I lifted up the stiff paper, slid my thumb under the adhesive and popped it open.

There were more symbols... just like the ones in the journal.

Bex leaned over. "Aren't those..."

"Yeah, they sure are. This is the code that I need to decipher the text."

"You know what it all means now?"

I shook my head. "No. I still need the frame of reference. It's in a language I don't understand. It's like trying to program a computer with duck calls. The computer recognizes you are making sounds but has no way to process them. I know this decodes the journal possibly, but I need to understand the source language before I'll be able to figure it out." I frowned. "What piece was it that broke?"

She checked the inventory list. "Lot 57834234. The one we got the call about the other day."

My body went cold. "Since that thing broke apart in your hand, what are the chances that they were really calling looking for this scroll and not the flimsy piece of art?"

"I would agree with that." She glanced at the door. "You think this is why you have your non-nanny guards?"

"Oh, I'm absolutely certain of it. What the fuck was Willa into?"

"It's okay. We'll figure it out. You're not alone, okay?"

I tried to drag in a deep breath. "Okay, you're right. It's fine. Everything is going to be fine."

But I didn't believe that, because just like when we were kids, Willa was still managing to get me into trouble.

I held tightly onto the scroll. "Yeah, so—" The lights cut off.

I heard Bex mutter, "Son of a bitch. You think she didn't pay the electric bill?"

I had no idea where the breaker was. And something told me that was going to become absolutely necessary.

All I heard was a voice. "Neela?"

"Yeah, back here."

Tamsin had a flashlight with her, and she located us right away.

Then she was tapping something in her ear. She whispered, "We have to go. Backdoor. Now. Zia is waiting in the car."

Something about the tone of her voice told me to shut the hell up and follow her without question. I grabbed my purse and laptop, and then we were moving. Bex, on the other hand, was whispering rapid fire at her. "Why do we have to go? We're not done."

Tamsin shot her a look that said, 'shut the hell up,' grabbed her arm, and pushed her toward the backdoor. She also turned off her flashlight. For someone with no light, she was excellent at navigating. By the time we managed to get to the backdoor, she tapped her ear piece one more time, held up a hand to let us know to stop, and then she counted, "Three, two, one," and pushed the backdoor open. The shrill alarm went off, and she was dragging us behind her, running, sprinting outside into the waiting car where Zia drove up with a screech.

Tamsin practically shoved the two of us in the backseat, and she lunged into the front.

Zia didn't even wait for us to close our doors before she was peeling away. It was a good thing too. Two men ran outside the backdoor seconds after us. They were big, and one of them looked familiar.

Had I seen him before? Both of them whipped out guns. The taller of the two took aim. The booming crack shattered the calm around them.

We weren't hit, but then it was harder to hit a moving target and Zia had wasted no time peeling out.

Hands shaking, I buckled my seatbelt and sputtered at Tamsin. "What the fuck?"

"Zia noticed a van that had been parked outside across the street. Been there since last night. We've had surveillance on the gallery, obviously. Zia ran the plates and they were stolen. As I got the call, the lights went out. So, I came for you guys, and told her to come around back."

"Holy shit. Someone is legitimately trying to hurt me."

"Was this what happened to Willa?" Bex asked.

Tamsin just shook her head. "I don't know. But we need to get Neela and Mayzie to safety quickly."

FOUR

JAX...

THE ANGEL and devil on my shoulders had been warring the last two days. The angel was convinced I'd brought this trouble on myself, and the devil, well, he thought I should kiss her and make up.

It didn't help that I'd been nearly certain I heard buzzing the other night. The only thing I knew that buzzed like that was a vibrator. A big one. So lucky me, my mind had conjured up all kinds of scenarios where she'd come to me to help her sleep.

Basically, every porn fantasy come to life.

There was a reason they called it fantasy. Because she'd never come to me. And as it was, she only spoke to me regarding Mayzie's care. As if I really was the damn manny.

I shouldn't have slept with her.

What I shouldn't have done was do every dirty thing I'd imagined doing to her from the moment I saw her. That's what I shouldn't have done.

But it was too late for that now. Because there was no going back. I hadn't been able to keep my bloody hands to myself. One look at her, and it had been over. So now she felt betrayed and pissed the hell off. As well she should.

I picked Mayzie up out of her car seat. She was fast asleep, but still I unlatched her, picked her up, and grabbed the diaper bag.

Ariel had called us all back to the house, and she wouldn't say why. When I stepped in the house, I understood why. Something had happened. My whole team was inside.

Trace nodded at me, immediately reaching for the baby, who had fallen asleep. "Let me put her down."

He nodded. "You know what's going on?"

I shook my head.

I was up the stairs and into the nursery in no time. On the way back, I ran into Neela coming out of the master bedroom. "Neela—"

"Don't talk to me."

Shit. I reached for her arm, and she snatched it back. "Don't talk to me. Don't touch me. Don't even look at me."

Fuck. "You think I wanted to lie to you?"

I knew she didn't want me touching her, but it was important that I deliver the message.

I stepped around and in front of her but kept my hands behind my back. I didn't want her to be afraid. That was the last thing I wanted. I dropped my voice. "I've said it, and I'll keep saying it. I never wanted to lie to you. I came here to take a job. Bodyguard. Simple. But the man who hired me insisted I not tell you I was your bodyguard. That was the job. I did it."

She tilted her chin up. "Oh, yeah? Was fucking me part of the job too?"

I winced. "You know it wasn't."

But she was on a roll. "Because wow, what a spectacular job

you did. I see you take your work seriously. Ariel should give you a raise. I didn't know she was running a bodyguard-gigolo agency."

That did it.

I took her hand, despite her not wanting any part of it, and turned her into the master bedroom. When I closed the door behind us, I regretted that decision. I was locked in with her scent now. All around us. I could feel her. Neela must have packed up all of Willa's things, because they were gone. Now there were pictures of Neela and Mayzie, and of Mayzie and Willa. But the scent that lingered, honey and lime, that was all Neela.

I wasn't going to make it. "Listen to me. What happened, it wasn't part of the plan. I tried to stop it from happening, remember?"

"You mean when you ghosted after you kissed me?"

"I did *not* ghost you." I dropped my voice. "I just realized it was a terrible fucking idea. I couldn't do my job and touch you."

"Yeah, but you changed your mind, didn't you?"

"Only because I couldn't *not* anymore. God, you think I want this? You think I *ever* wanted this?"

"Tell me? Would it have been easier to control me once you slept with me? Was it getting too difficult, me running around, too hard to guard?"

"That's asinine."

She stepped around me and reached for the door. "You know what's asinine? Me believing that you or someone like you could've fallen for me. I know, my dumb mistake. I won't make it again."

She was out the door in seconds, and I was chasing after her again. But before I could call out her name, Tamsin was already up the stairs. "There you two are. Come on, we don't have much time. We need to talk about this."

I groaned and followed behind the two of them.

Trace, ever watchful, narrowed his gaze at me and then flicked his dark eyes to Neela and back again. Then he gave me a shit-eating grin. *Asshole.*

Once we were all downstairs, Ariel took the floor. "Listen up guys, we don't have much time. Someone shot at Neela at the gallery."

My gaze darted to Neela. Shit. She looked fine. Was she fine? Mother fucker. I should've been with her.

Ariel was still talking. "Given what Neela's told us, this incident is very likely related to the ledger. To catch you up Jax, Neela basically found the secret decoder ring." She turned her attention to Neela. "Is that the right way to explain it?"

Neela nodded. "Yeah. This scroll apparently has the cypher code on it. The problem is I still don't know the language, but I can keep working on it."

Ariel shook her head. "You're gonna have to work on it on the road."

She frowned. "What?"

Ariel shook her head. "Look, they were waiting for you. You can't go to the gallery. And anyone who knows who your clients are will be staking them out too. Which means you can't go see any of your clients, which means you can't do your job."

Neela threw up her hands. "Then what the hell am I supposed to do?"

"Put things on hold. Your safety is paramount. Mayzie's safety is paramount."

"But I have a business to run."

I didn't even realize that Adam and Bex were in the room

until Adam spoke up. "Actually, Neela, as long as you have access to your laptop and an encrypted line, you can work remotely. I can do the client meetings. No one wants to hurt me."

Zia darted a glance at him, and I could see it in her eyes. She very much wanted him. But that was another problem for another day.

"Adam I can't just ask you to—"

He shook his head. "Look. When doucheface was being, well a doucheface, you didn't ask for my help then. When he was busy stealing your clients and stealing your employees, you didn't let me say anything. At least let me do this. You know how good I am. I can manage it. As long as they find out who's doing this soon, between Bex and I, we've got it handled."

Bex looked up. "He's right. We got you. All you have to do is ask for some help."

She rolled her shoulders. "You guys. You don't need to do this."

But neither one of them was listening to her.

They were already chattering about how they were going to shuffle things.

Ariel nodded. "Okay, we'll put someone on you guys to make sure you're covered while you work as if nothing's changed."

Neela held her hand up. "I'm sorry, are we making decisions without me again? I am done with that. This is my show."

Ariel sighed and stepped in front of her. "I'm sorry, Neela. But it's not. Bipps is running the show. And if you want what's best for Mayzie, it's not staying here."

Neela scowled. "That man has been interfering with my life far too long."

"Well I think he's trying to keep you safe. Well, at least keep Mayzie safe. You're her guardian, and she can't go without you. And honestly, I think they're after you and that journal. Whatever's in it is valuable, dangerous information. You need protection. And while you figure out what's in that journal, I think the safest place for you isn't here. Anyone who was watching Willa or has ever been in the house is a potential threat. I'd prefer you were somewhere safer."

Neela sighed, her shoulders slumping. "Where am I supposed to go?"

"We have a safe house on King's Island. You'll take Jax with you."

Neela did a double take "What? Hell, no."

Ariel shrugged. "I'm sorry, but I'm gonna put Trace and Jameson on Bex and Adam. Zia just got here, but I've already got her on a client. And I need Tamsin to help try and figure out who these people are."

"Give me Jameson. You take him." She darted her glare in my direction.

Ariel shrugged. "I'm sorry. I know you're mad at him, but you shouldn't be. He did it under orders. But he's the best with Mayzie. And he knows the case better than anyone else. I'd be happy to switch out if you were that uncomfortable. But he's the best you have right now."

Neela said nothing else, but I could see her shoulders stiffening. Fantastic, she was resigned. "Whatever."

Ariel nodded brusquely. "Good. You leave tonight."

The guilt ate at me. Gnawed at me. I'd done this. I'd shattered her world, and I knew what that felt like. I knew how she felt. It was unavoidable.

That's because you couldn't keep your dick in your pants.

I'd wanted her too much, and now we were both going to pay for it.

♛

Neela...

WHY ARE YOU MAD? Deep down you knew he wasn't a manny.

Had I known?

Once the decision was made, Jax didn't say a word. Upstairs, with brisk efficiency though, he packed up Mayzie. Clothes, diapers, enough to last for several weeks.

While he did that, and apparently Tamsin and Bex went to pack me up, the rest of the Royal Elite team was picking apart my house.

Don't you mean Willa's house?

Right, Willa's house.

"Did anyone else notice that these are bulletproof?" Trace asked, tapping on one of the windows.

Jax called out from the playroom as he managed to pick her four favorite toys. "Yeah, I noticed that the first day we were here."

I frowned. "Bulletproof? Why? Willa wouldn't know how to get something bulletproofed." Actually, scratch that. Knowing what I knew about Willa now, she would absolutely know.

Ariel slipped me a gaze over the top of her laptop. "Just how well did you know Willa MacKenzie?"

"Look, in the last couple years or so, we haven't been close. Ever since she got pregnant with Mayzie. She was still partying pretty hard, and maybe I was asking too many questions and judging. I don't know. We had a big fight. I told her that she was having a baby and she needed to be responsible, and she pretty much cut me out of her life after that. We hadn't spoken since then. I was more shocked than anybody when she named me as Mayzie's guardian."

Ariel nodded and went back to typing.

I glanced around. Zia was the only one giving me a sympathetic look.

From her bouncing walker thingy, Mayzie babbled and threw a block.

Trace smiled down at her, scooted down to her eye level, and handed her block back to her. She rewarded him with one of her Mayzie grins and then threw it again.

He shook his head. "I'm basically playing catch with the baby."

Jax tucked several ice packs into one of the bags, and then he took a whole armful of the baby food from the pantry. "Well, at least she knows you're a dog."

Trace mumbled. "Hey, I resemble that remark. I'm terrible for dating, but awesome for babies."

Mayzie seemed to adore Trace. Yeah well, who could blame the girl?

"Someone needs to tell me what's happening and why it's happening please."

Everyone was silent, and all gazes turned to Ariel, except for Jax's because he was busy packing. In the other room, Jameson was on security screen duty. On the smaller flat screen, she had on reruns of *Star Trek*.

Jax picked Mayzie up from the walker, and she happily slapped both her hands on his cheeks. He made a face at her, but it wasn't his usual soft-eyed one. This one was harsher. More defined steel. He was tense. Worried.

It was Ariel who spoke to me. "Okay, I'm sorry. I know that this is tough. A whole team of people are at work, and no one is telling you what the fuck is going on. I get it." She slid a glance to the baby. "Sorry."

I shrugged.

"It looks like your friend Willa was into some bad shit. She was helping criminals launder money through her art gallery."

"Bipps already gave me that information. I still don't know why anyone would come after me or Mayzie? I had nothing to do with this."

Ariel's voice was soft. "I know." She tucked her hands into the front pockets of her pants. "But you and little miss over there inherited everything. Not to mention you're the only one likely smart enough to decipher what the journal says."

I swallowed. "I'm working on it." I was still undecided if I was going to tell them when I figured it out.

She pursed her lips. "Maybe we should put it somewhere for safe keeping. I don't want to risk it getting into the wrong hands. Can you quickly photograph the pages?"

I nodded. "Yeah, that's a good idea." I'd already made my own copies. But Ariel could have her own if she wanted.

"The point is, the two of you are sitting ducks here. You'd be better off in a safe house. We have one on King's Island. You'll be safe there until we can decipher the ledger and find who's behind this. I promise, Jax will keep you two safe and the rest of us will take good care of your team. You don't have to worry."

"My whole life is in upheaval now."

"I know. Believe, me I know. But what's more important?

Your job or your life?" She inclined her head toward Mayzie. "Maybe hers?"

My heart squeezed as I watched Mayzie play in Jax's arms. His gaze met mine again, and he nodded. "Nothing is going to happen to you. Your team is in good hands and they can hold down the fort."

In the end, I had no choice. I would have to trust them.

Trust him.

Neela...

THE LAST THING on earth I wanted was to leave my team behind. But Ariel was right. We were sitting ducks there. Mayzie especially. If no one knew where we were, she'd at least be safe.

In the safety of our office, I gave them the rundown of how things would work while I was gone. "I'm not sure how long I'll be gone. But we'll have sat phones, and I'll be in touch every couple of days."

Bex gave me a tight hug. "We'll be fine. As long as that hottie Trace is the one guarding my body."

No matter what, Bex could always put me on the brink of a smile. "At least one of us will be getting something good out of this."

From behind his monitor, Adam fist pumped. "Tell me how much you love me."

I glowered at Adam. "I don't have time for this. The body-guard say it's time to go."

Bex sat up. "Did they tell you where?"

"No, they won't tell me. But after what happened at the gallery, it's not exactly safe for Mayzie."

Bex frowned, but she nodded. "No, I get it. That was terrifying. If they hadn't been there, we would have been in deep shit."

"Adam, what did you find?"

"It's just a start, but I was going through known languages for the ledger and coming up with nothing. Then I just read an article on how some companies use languages from books to create ciphers."

"You mean like Elvish from Tolkien—" suddenly I stopped. Earlier, back at the house, the television had been on. "Screw the book languages. Try television. *Star Trek* to be exact."

He frowned. "Are you serious right now?"

My heart rate kicked up. "Yes. I've been wondering why some of those symbols looked so familiar. Earlier one of the *Star Trek* movies was on. They were speaking Klingon. Some of the symbols on the Klingon ship looked familiar."

Adam's eyes went wide. "One, you're amazing. Two, who knew you were a closet nerd?"

"Duh, I'm a cryptanalyst who loves puzzles."

"I'm on it."

I ran through client protocols with Bex quickly only to look up and see Adam had started dancing. "You are a genius. A quick cross reference and I found an article Vanhorn was interviewed for a few years ago. He talks about how he learned to read from watching dubbed *Star Trek* episodes. He's a huge sci-fi fan."

"Bingo. You and the computer get to work."

He grinned again. "It somehow makes me oddly happy that Vanhorn is also a total nerd."

"Look who's talking."

He snorted a laugh. “Says the woman who knew to look at *Star Trek*.”

"Wait, *Star Wars* and *Star Trek* are the same thing, right?"

Adam just blinked at me, jaw unhinged. "What? Please tell me you know the difference between *Star Trek* and *Star Wars*. If you don't, just pretend. *Lie* to me."

I laughed. "Yes, I know the difference. You should see your face."

“Not funny. I’ve got the computer keyed in, but that's going to take at least a few hours."

I ran my hands through my hair. "Okay. I need to get back to the main house. I’ll check in soon okay?"

“You got it.

I nodded. "Bex, as soon as Adam finishes deciphering half of that, I want you to take the translations and hide them. Obviously, keep a copy, but hide them."

Bex sat up. "Hiding shit. That's my purview."

I nodded. "Yeah. Take it to the yoga studio on Queen Ave. The one that advertises that you can find your inner queen when doing yoga there. There’s a panel behind the tampons. Willa used to hide party drugs in there when she worked there. Figured if a cop ever got wind of what she was doing, they’d never look there."

She frowned. "Are you serious?"

“Yeah, that was Willa. I only knew about it because she was schmoozing some actress and brought her to the studio for a class. Then she took her to the bathroom to pick out her drugs.” I shook my head. “That was probably the beginning of the end of our friendship. She’d veered way off the path at that point. Most of that stuff was recreational pills, but none of that was me. I didn’t want to be on that train when it finally wrecked.”

Bex sighed. "Jesus, she was such a damn mess."

"Yeah well, she hid it really well. To the outside world, Willa was damn near perfect."

She and Adam exchanged a glance. But it was Adam who asked, "Are you sure you don't want to clue the bodyguard in that we're close to figuring this shit out?"

Maybe at some point. But not now. "No. I want you to continue working at it. I'll do what I can with my laptop, but as soon as we have pages, even a third of it, go hide it. At this point, I have learned the hard way not to trust anyone. You guys are it. As soon as you have anything workable, let me know."

Adam nodded. "You got it, boss. Listen, if you really do have to leave, please be careful. I don't trust that guy."

"That makes two of us."

Bex just rolled her eyes. "Look, I personally say hear the guy out."

"He said plenty. I'm in no mood to hear him out for any reason."

Bex nodded. "I know. He was a complete and total douche. He deserves all of your wrath. But if you're going to be stuck with him, you're going to have to find a way to trust him."

"I trust him when it comes to Mayzie. Anything beyond that, it's a pipe dream. And also irresponsible."

Bex shrugged. "If you say so. I'm just saying, if you want any girl chat, you can reach me on the app."

"That's if they even let me have access to it. Right now, I need to do what's best for Mayzie, which means getting the hell out of dodge. But you guys keep working and figure it out. As soon as we have some answers, maybe I'll be able to secure all of our freedom."

FIVE

KING SEBASTIAN...

My UNCLE LOOKED OLDER than I remembered.

In the bright sunshine of his patio on the villa overlooking the water, he looked like an old man.

He looks like he should be king.

Except, I was king because of a decision he'd made before I was even born.

"Uncle Roland, thank you for agreeing to see me."

He pushed himself to stand as he smiled at me. "Sebastian."

He started to kneel, but I rushed forward and grabbed him by the shoulders. "Uncle, stop it. You of all people do not kneel before me. That's not how this goes."

His smile was kind. His green eyes crinkled at the corners. "I am one of your subjects. I should kneel before my king."

"Not when you were king first."

"Are we going to argue this all afternoon?"

I squared my shoulders. "I'm prepared to."

He shook his head and took a seat, inclining his head and offering me one next to him.

The brightly colored umbrella provided adequate shade.

Off in the distance, I could hear children playing down at the beach. Staff scurried about, bringing out refreshments. In so many ways, this villa tucked away in Mallorca reminded me so much of home.

It had been in the family since before I was born, and I'd spent a lot of time here on school vacations.

"I hope you'll forgive my surprise intrusion."

He waved a hand. "This is your villa. It's not an intrusion. Everything I have is because of your generosity."

I winced. I certainly didn't want a reminder that my uncle was here because of me in any way. "Are you well?"

He nodded slowly. "Me and your aunt... well, I'm well. She's... resigned to her new lot in life."

I shook my head. "How did everything get so messy?"

I had never known my uncle as king, but I'd spent a good amount of time in his company when I was younger. I'd always known him as warm and kind. I'd always assumed he regretted giving up the throne, but he'd never seemed jealous of my father. That blatant animosity I felt from my oldest cousin, Ashton, I never sensed from my uncle. Not once. While there were some who would have killed to be king, he was far happier being normal.

"Well, everything has always been messy, especially when it comes to who sits on the throne. To outsiders looking in, it looks pristine and beautiful. They think it's all relaxing days at court eating peeled grapes. But behind the curtain, it's ugly and dark, and sometimes bloody. That is why I stepped aside. I didn't have the constitution for it."

"You know, I'm not sure my father did either."

His smile was kind. "You saw him through a boy's eyes. The man was quite capable. And he had your mother beside him.

Yes, they had a rocky start, obviously, but once they locked in together, he had a rock. And that was good for him. He was always supposed to sit on the throne. I just had the unfortunate luck of birth order."

"And me? What's my excuse?"

He leveled a stern gaze on me. "You are your father's son."

Fuck, I hoped so. Sometimes I wondered if I was strong enough to rule. "I am so sorry you are even here. You should be in your quarters in the palace, enjoying your old age."

He shrugged. "I have beautiful sunshine, pristine beaches... what's the difference what country it's in?"

It did make a damn difference. "Uncle Roland, the Winston Isles is your home."

"Of course, it is. It always has been. It always will be. But home isn't your address. You know this. It's what is in your heart. Maybe one day I'll be able to return. But maybe I shouldn't. I hate that my family caused yours so much pain."

"It's all the same family."

"Yes, and no. Your aunt, even though she wasn't directly involved, her affair... of course, I knew about it. Back then, you did what you had to do to hide it. And I wasn't king anymore, so it should have been easy, but there were a lot of mistakes made. Ones I wish I could rectify."

When everything had broken about the conspiracy, how the descendants of my great-great uncle thought they were the ones in line for the throne, I hadn't had a chance to really speak to my uncle. The Council had shunned him and my aunt and my two cousins. Ashton, their first born, was already exiled for trying to hurt Penny. His exile just happened to come with prison guards too.

They'd all been given one Royal Guard each and a meager

stipend. But they'd been succinctly erased, as if such a thing was even possible. It was as if everyone in the palace wanted to pretend they didn't exist. It had been a tidy job, a tidy clean-up. But nothing about the situation was clean.

"I just wish there was more I could have done. It's just a strange thing being king and not being in charge."

"Ah, yes, the Council. They mean well. But more often than not, I honestly thought they meant well for themselves."

"Sometimes I get that impression too. Although, there are two seats coming up for vote, and I need to fill them with my sister and Roone."

"Don't waste one on your sister. Remember that as a child of Cassius, she deserves one. Ask Ethan. There's an ancient loophole. It's there though. Just because she's female, doesn't mean she doesn't get a seat."

I frowned. "Okay. In that case, I'll need to find someone else. Are you looking for a job, Uncle?"

He laughed then. "No, I'm retired. I'm tired, son." His eyes were warm. "I always wished you were my son. I mean, you were a hell-raiser to be sure, but there was always something kind and good-hearted about you. And maybe that was the problem. I always compared Ashton to you, and somehow, I was always disappointed."

Just the mention of my cousin set my teeth on edge. "Have you been to see him?"

"I went once, to ask him why. Why he would get into bed with that lot. Why he had so much hate in his heart."

"Did you get the answers you were looking for?"

"No, I didn't. Not that I actually ever expected them. And as for Alix, and Tristan, I see them every couple of months. Tristan came out here, sat exactly where you are sitting, and we chatted.

Then he had to run off for a game or a practice or something. Alix comes more often. She doesn't live a life in the public eye, obviously, but she misses home."

I nodded. "She should be able to come home. The exile isn't mandatory."

"No, it's not. And we all know that, but we know about the optics. My oldest son tried to kill you and the current queen. My wife had an affair that produced a son who very much thought *he* was the heir, and also that he could kill you. You can understand how the Council doesn't exactly want us back, right?"

"Well, when you put it like that."

He chuckled low. "No, I don't need to return, but Alix and Tristan should be able to. It's their home. I lived my whole life there. I'm an old man now. I carry the Winston Isles in my heart. They're young. They just want to return."

"I'm working on it. But, Uncle, obviously I came to ask a question."

"Go on, I know. As much as I enjoy visiting with you, I know how busy you are. And you didn't come with your beautiful wife, so I know this must be urgent."

"I already asked Ethan to look for an answer. The best historian on the island is on the Council, and I obviously don't want to alert anyone to what I'm trying to do, but I wanted to know if you had any information on creating King's Knights."

His eyes went wide. "Oh, my goodness. You really do think that the Council can't be trusted."

I ground my teeth. "They won't provide an extra guard for Tris."

My uncle's lips formed a thin line. "The shooting, I knew he was down playing it."

"He has to be. I went to see him. He looked fine, but he needs to have more than one guard."

"Yes, and the Council won't provide it. And they're not obligated to. They're playing politics. Each vying to kiss your ass the hardest."

"And by doing that, they're doing what's *not* in my best interest."

"Tell them that."

"Oh, I did. I was outvoted."

His brows slid up again. "Even with all your votes? And your mother? And Lucas, Ethan, Penny. You were still outvoted?"

"Yes. They all voted to not provide additional security for him, or Alix, or you. Of course, Ashton is basically in prison, so that's a whole other thing. Frankly, I think the Council has members who aren't to be trusted. With two more seats, I can affect a lot of change. But I can still get outvoted. And with everything shaping up how it is, it concerns me. If they deemed me unfit for any reason, they could try and remove me."

"Oh, no. After what's happened, you're safe for now. It will take at least ten years before someone gets a wild hair up their ass that you don't belong on the throne. Right now, they know it will be unpopular with people, so they won't risk it."

I nodded for him to continue.

"So, about the Knights... I mean, even by the time our father was king, it was always the Council and the Royal Guard. And the time before that, during your grandfather's reign, that was when they started to merge. It was like there were two security forces. The military arm and the king's private army that he alone commanded. But the Council wanted more power because your grandfather made them uncomfortable. And in your great-grandfather's time, some of the Knights went rogue." He sighed. "The Council thought your grandfather could mount enough private guards to force the removal of the Council. At the end of the day, he could have if he'd wanted to. So, they did away with the King's Knights. But the law states that the king is entitled to his own private Knights to direct as only he sees fit. The Council doesn't rule them."

"How do I do it?"

"It's fairly easy, honestly. It's just that everyone has forgotten about it. With the Royal Guard acting more like secret service, it wasn't even necessary. But if you want your own King's Knights, they're at your disposal. You just have to create them. Ask Ethan to look in the archives of Jackson. He should find all the paperwork there. You're the king. You have a political arm, yes, that's your Council. But you can still make these choices. The Knights are yours."

"The Knights are mine."

He nodded. "Let me guess. You're looking to scare the Council and use Knights to protect your cousin?"

"I know it's transparent, but they're being stupid."

He grinned. "I couldn't agree more.

Ariel...

BY THE TIME I reached headquarters, my neck hurt, and my head throbbed. But for now, Mayzie MacKenzie and Neela Wellbrook were safe. I had taken them to the ferry myself.

Jax was taking them to the safe house, and he'd check in once they landed safely. Tamsin was staying on site with Adam and Bex for the night. Trace was on our other bodyguard job for an event. The rest of the team was off-shift.

When I walked in, I hit the alarm code and reset it as soon as the door was locked behind me. I tossed my keys on the mantle by the door, and then I went straight into the kitchen where I found a chilled white wine. "Oh my God, heaven." There was a Post-it on it. The note read, 'You look tired. Have a glass. Try and relax. We got this. -- Zia.'

"Oh my God, I love that woman."

I 'd grabbed some food at Neela's, but a glass of wine was just what I needed. After I uncorked the wine and poured a glass, I headed straight back to my room. As soon as I was in my door, the shoes came off, the blazer came off, and I sank back onto the bed, careful not to tip my glass too much.

I pulled my phone from my back pocket and dialed, listening to the ring as I called Penny.

She answered on the third ring. "Sorry. Sorry. You know me, I was painting. There was nowhere to put my phone."

I chuckled softly. "I loved that nothing ever changes."

"Are you okay? You sound, I don't know, sad?"

I pinched the bridge of my nose. She knew me too well. "No, I'm fine. Just stressed out. Someone is trying to kill a client. You know how it is."

She cursed under her breath. "Do you need back up?"

I almost laughed at the headlines playing in my head. 'Queen Penelope shoots armed guard.'

"Oh my God, you cannot give me back up. You are the Queen of the Winston Isles."

"I'm also a goddamn Royal Guard. And I'm cooped up in the palace."

"You know that sounds so bougie, right? Oh no, my palace."

She laughed. "I know. I sound ridiculous, but I *am* cooped up. I think I'm due for another visit. Want me to come down? I'll rustle up some guards. See, look at me following directions."

I laughed. "Let me guess, Sebastian wanted you to take a forty-man team and you refused?"

"I mean, the man is ridiculous. *Forty men*. I can go under cover of night and no one would even see me."

Please, God, no. Sebastian would kill me. He was a bit ridiculous about Penny's safety. "Yes, you have done that before. But remember how well that turned out?"

"Oh yeah, I got the shag of my life."

I groaned. "No, Penny. That's not what I mean. He was *pissed*."

"Yes. But still, I got the shag of my life."

"I would rather not hear about you and king shagging if you don't mind."

"What? I seem to recall a time when you would pump me for details."

"Yes, but that was before I got to know him better, and he was just, you know, abs and a really great ass. Now it's gross."

She laughed. "No, I'm trying to do better. We'd been working on our communication. We negotiated down to five guards."

"Five, now that sounds more reasonable."

"I know, right? Not that I even need a guard, but whatever."

"How many times do I have to tell you, you are the queen now."

"It's just hard. It was like the one thing I did not anticipate, some of my independence being gone."

"Honey, I'm sorry."

"Never mind my moaning in my gilded tower. What's wrong with you, besides someone trying to kill your client?"

"Nothing. I'm just checking in. Long day. I had to put the client in a safe house until we can figure out who's trying to kill her. She's pissed we lied about being nannies. And I think she's shagging Jax."

"Jax... the hot British one? I don't blame her."

I snorted a laugh. "I mean objectively, neither do I. He's stupid hot, but I gave him one rule...not to shag her. That didn't stop those two, though. I mean, I knew as soon as they saw each other they were gonna do it and ruin my company before it even started."

"Now who's being melodramatic? You're not ruined. You'll keep her safe. Isn't that what you do?"

"I don't know. After Jessa, everything feels off. I feel like my instincts aren't working. I missed my father's betrayal. So, what if I'm missing other things?" My father had been part of the conspiracy to take down the royal family. He'd jeopardized my life and freedom and tried to hurt my friends. In the end, I'd been the one to take him down.

"Is it terrible that we have become accustomed to this by now? Oh, someone is just shooting at the royal family. La di da..."

I laughed. "You know what? It has become a little commonplace. Maybe we need new lines of work."

She clucked. "Never. So, have you um, heard from anyone?"

I knew what she was asking. "Oh my God, Penny, you're not even trying to be subtle."

"It's okay to be curious, or if you look him up, or if you tried to contact him. I know you said no, but after that whole thing in Austria..."

Did I tell the truth? "I mean, I still have my Google alert on."

"I knew it. You're not totally over him."

"But I need to be because it hurts me."

There was a bit of silence. "I'm sorry. If it's hurting you, then I will try to help you get over it."

"But it kind of hurts in a good way."

She chuckled. "Please do not let us have this relationship where I'm the voice of reason now."

She had a point there. "Never."

"I mean, how long has it been since you saw him?"

"Well, basically, ten years. I'm just worried that he's okay."

"I think Sebastian is talking to his uncle to see if there is a way around the Council. I suggested they have Knights. You know, like the Knights of the Round Table."

"Oh my God, your Arthurian fascination is ridiculous."

"I love that, but whatever. Apparently, the Royal Guards used to be Knights. There was the policing arm, and then the king's personal guard. Sebastian was telling me the history after he left his uncle's villa. So, I guess there's a way to do it and what not." Penny said nonchalantly.

"Well, that will be perfect. And then they'd get around the pesky 'no civilians-guarding-royalty' thing. I hope it works. Tristan might have treated me like dirt, but I certainly don't want him to die."

"That hardly sounds like you. You're the first one who was like, 'murder the assholes.'"

"I know. I mellowed in my old age."

"You're barely twenty-seven."

"I'm twenty-six," I huffed. "My birthday is still not for three months."

She laughed. "I know, and I've got the best thing planned. Oh my God, we're going to have a 90's-themed party."

I shook my head. "Oh my God, Penny, I am regretting this already."

"It's going to be epic."

"Wait, aren't I supposed to be the one planning ridiculous parties and saying they're going to be epic, and you groan and go, 'Oh no. Please no, not that epic party?'"

"You're just tense. Why don't you come up tomorrow and if you can, we'll have a girls' night?"

"I wish I could. I've got to keep an eye on the situation here. Maybe this weekend?"

"You've got a deal. And look, it's perfectly natural to be curious about him. I still think you need to talk to him, because there is no getting closure without it. It's just like this open, festering wound, you know?"

"No, no festering. It's just a mild, annoying scratch."

"If you say so. But even scratches can get infected. So maybe if you just call him up and say, 'Hey, that was a douche-canoe move that one time,' then you can let him go finally."

"Never going to happen." Except the thing was the more times she said it, the more times I wondered if that was exactly what I needed.

SIX

JAX…

SHE WAS SCARED. I could tell. She'd been practically silent on the ferry to King's Island. Luckily, Mayzie had slept for most of it. She woke up and fussed a little bit, but when I gave her binky to her, it soothed her right back to sleep.

There was no binky for Neela, though.

Oh yeah, there is.

Fuck. I adjusted my position to make my growing erection less prominent.

No. How I could even think about sex right now, was beyond me. We were in real shit. Real people were trying to kill her. This was not just some run-of-the-mill protection job. No, something could have happened to her.

By the time we reached the safehouse, I could tell her nerves were shot. I punched in the security code, and the gates swung open. While it was called a bungalow, it was a good deal bigger than one and sat on about a quarter of an acre.

As safehouses went, it was nice. Decently furnished with a bright airy feel because of all the damn windows.

Did Ariel know about the damn windows? How was I going to keep the place safe? I shot off a quick text.

Jax: *Arrived safe. House full of windows.*

Her response was immediate.

Ariel: *Bullet Proof. Also, cameras everywhere. Check security room.*

Okay, so I'd have a good vantage point. I knew from the schematics that there was a small pool on the premises, so at least Mayzie could get outside. And the village was close if we needed anything.

Neela paced the small living room. She looked out the window, went to take a look at the kitchen, and then headed to check on Mayzie, who was in the bedroom. When she completed the circuit, then she would start all over again.

"I know. It feels like a cage."

She glanced around. "Well, it is a very nice cage."

I shrugged. "Tell that to Ariel. It's a Royal Elite safehouse, I guess."

"Is it true she worked for the king?"

I nodded. "Yeah, she did."

"That's prestigious company to keep. I assume you were a Guard too?"

I nodded, acknowledging the elephant in the room. "I was."

She shook her head. "I don't know a thing about you."

I ran my hand through my hair. "Yes, you do. You know the important things."

"Not the fundamental things that make you you."

"What, like my job? You know why I left the island."

She shook her head. "It doesn't matter."

"For what it's worth, I'm sorry. I wish it could have gone down differently. I wish to Christ when I saw you I didn't feel like I'd been bloody poleaxed in my sternum. I couldn't breathe when I looked at you. You stunned me. That's the truth. And even though I knew not to touch you... Fuck, I tried. I tried so hard. And I failed. You asked me to kiss you, and that was the nail in my coffin of restraint. I couldn't say no."

"God, I must have looked so desperate."

I shook my head. "No. Just like a woman who wanted me as much as I wanted her."

She cleared her throat. "Not happening again."

I narrowed my gaze at her. "You sure about that?" I planted my hands on the counter. "You still want me."

"You're a liar."

"It doesn't matter because you know why I had to do it. It's just an excuse for you to hide again."

She blinked rapidly. Her dark eyes narrowing. "We're not doing this. I need to try to work on the journal."

"If you say so. You know I'm not going to let anything happen to you, right?"

"You can't promise that."

"No, I can't make you a hundred percent guarantee, but I *will* protect you with my life."

"Giving your life for mine is not something I want."

Neela...

MAYZIE WAS FEELING cooped up too. She slept fitfully, which meant I was groggy and tired in the morning. When I woke up and shuffled into the kitchen, there was no sign of Jax, which made me feel both better and somehow worse.

I hit the button on the coffee maker and pulled out, despite myself, two mugs. Just because he was a lying ass didn't mean he didn't deserve coffee. Besides, he'd been up as much as I was with Mayzie.

For a man who wasn't actually a manny, he was really, really good with her.

As the scent of coffee wafted through the air, I leaned against the table and peered out the window, taking a good look at our surroundings. The house sat at the center of about a quarter-acre. The property was fenced, which was nice. We could basically see anybody coming for miles. And sure enough, by the large oak near the garage, there was Jax. And he was... dear God, the man was shirtless.

Yes, I knew what he looked like naked. I had spent a pleasurable evening just running my fingers over his washboard abs. But somehow, seeing those abs now that I couldn't have them was nerve-racking.

My skin was itchy and tight, and something deep and low in my belly coiled tight. God, he was beautiful. The sun shone on his shoulders, making his sweat glisten. He was on his stomach, somehow planting his hand beneath him and then lifting up his body into a... was that a plank? It was some kind of a gymnastics move. I'd seen it done before, but Jax was huge. Six foot four maybe, and he could do that? The pure control of his body was amazing.

Oh, you know that control.

He had held me up easily as he made love to me against the wall. He hadn't even looked winded.

When he eased out of the plank position and then stood, I quickly busied myself with the coffee. I added a mountain of sugar to mine and left his black. When he walked in the back door, he gave me a nod. "Good morning. How much sleep did you get?"

I held up the cup of coffee. "About as much as you did."

"Yeah, I'm sure it will get easier. At least she's asleep now. I figure we'll all establish a new routine while we're here."

"Yeah, we need to get her back on some kind of schedule, but for now she might as well sleep. Hell, if I can manage it, I want a nap. Coffee and a little bit of work first though."

His gaze tracked me. "Were you watching me through the window?"

I sputtered my coffee. "What?"

"Were you watching me?" His gaze met mine as he took a sip.

"You wish."

"What you don't seem to get is, I can feel you. That's why I knew we were sort of inevitable. From the moment I saw you in your office, there was no avoiding you. There was no running, no hiding. We were unavoidable. I can feel you watching me. It's like a caress. The moment you came out here and saw me out the window, I knew. I know exactly how long you've been watching me."

"You're so full of shit." When in doubt, deny, deny, deny. Lie your face off.

"You can say what you want. You and I both know the truth."

"Do you do this with all your women? Pester them until they talk to you?"

"Well, it's working so far, isn't it?"

"No, it's not. I have nothing else to say to you."

He grinned at me then. "Okay, if you say so."

He sauntered out of the kitchen, presumably to take a

shower, and I called after him. "When you come out, can you please put some clothes on?"

His chuckle was low and rolled over me and through me, making my chest hum and my nipples tight. "Why, is it bothering you?"

"No, I'm completely unbothered. You, on the other hand, are making a spectacle, and it's just sad."

I could still hear him laughing as he went into the bathroom and closed the door. As soon as he was out of earshot, I slumped against the counter.

Hell, that man was everything. If I was going to manage to exert some power over our dynamic, I was really going to need him to wear a shirt. Or I was going to be doomed.

SEVEN

NEELA...

WHILE JAX WAS FEEDING MAYZIE, I stepped out into the sunroom and slid the sliding glass door closed behind me. If he was curious as to what I was doing, he didn't ask any questions. I had the sat phone, as it was the protocol. I punched in the numbers and waited. Bex answered on the second ring.

"Hey, it's me. How are you guys doing?"

I could almost hear her sigh of relief. "Oh my God. You're good?"

"Yes, we sent a text when we got here. Didn't anyone tell you?"

"Well, they did, but I don't trust them. They could have been lying. They could have buried your body somewhere."

I rolled my eyes. "Bex, you're being ridiculous."

"Well, you said yourself, they lied and infiltrated our happy family."

"Yes, that is true."

"I'm putting Adam on speaker."

Adam's smooth timbre came on the line, and I had to smile at that. "Hey, boss lady."

"Hey yourself. Are you guys okay?"

"Yeah, we're good. It's a little weird not being able to go home, but yeah, this house is huge, so I feel like I practically have my own wing, like it's a hotel. Except, no one brings me breakfast in bed. No one brings me room service. It doesn't matter how many times I ask Jameson. I'm pretty sure if I ask her again though, she will scalp me."

"Oh my God, you're not hitting on her, are you?"

I could almost hear the grin in his voice. "Of course, not. I just merely said that I heard she was a badass and she should tell me if she wants me to make a move sometime."

Bex laughed. "Oh my God, you should have seen her face. I mean, the look she gave him was like he was something on a petri dish."

"She's just warming up to me. She'll come around. They always do."

I always wondered why Adam never seemed to have any luck with women. He was good looking, after all. Clearly brilliant. Maybe the whole problem was he had zero game.

"How are you guys coming on the ledger?"

Adam sighed. "There's a lot more data in there than I thought. This guy was an extra-nerd. Like we talked about, it's Klingon for sure, but there are other elements. Some I don't recognize. I'm still working on it."

"God save me from my fellow super-nerd. At least we know what lexicon he's using."

"It's a big start. We've got about a quarter of it deciphered. There is so much data. We might need more processing power."

I swore. "Wow. This guy was serious. Any of the data make sense yet?"

Bex chimed in then. "No, not yet. Right now, we have pieces of names here and there, but we'll get there."

"Anything you translate, make sure that you're storing it somewhere safe."

"You got it boss," Adam said. "So where are you exactly?" There was a hint of worry in Adam's voice.

"I'm safe. That's pretty much all I think I'm allowed to say. I mean, I can't help but say that it feels a little bit like we're in prison."

Adam asked nervously, "We're sure these guys are the good guys, right?"

I could practically hear Bex rolling her eyes. "Of course, they're the good guys. Because how many movies have we seen, where what seems like the good guys are really the bad guys?"

I couldn't help my laugh. "You think everything is a Michael Bay movie. They're annoying, but they're the good guys."

Adam sighed. "How do you know that? All because Bex said so?"

"Well now that I know who they are, I looked them up. They actually do check out."

He didn't miss a beat. "Didn't they check out the last time we checked them out?"

"That is beside the point Adam. The point is, if they wanted to hurt me or you guys, they could have by now."

"No, they couldn't have. We didn't have the ledger figured out."

That gave me a chill deep down. He had a point there. It would certainly explain a lot. But someone had tried to grab me off the street. Jax stopped them, and he'd very deliberately not killed them. Unless, that was one of their own men?

"No. You're going to make me paranoid. Once I knew where

to look, I could see Ariel in the background of pictures with the king and queen."

"Those can be doctored."

I pinched the bridge of my nose. "Adam, enough with the conspiracy theories, okay? Just keep working on the ledger. Call me when you have something."

"Okay, I will. I'm just telling you to be careful, okay?"

"Yes, of course. I'm always careful."

Then he tossed in. "Don't bone your hot bodyguard."

"Adam!"

"Look, Bex certainly was not going to say it. But after he lied and all that jazz, maybe you needed a friend who was going to tell you to just not do it."

I sighed. "I promise. It's not going to happen."

There was a beat of silence. "Did you say that to yourself before you did it the last time, or...?"

"Adam! You work for me."

"Yeah, but you know, we're also friends, so it kind of needs to be said. You need to look out for yourself. A guy like him, I don't know. I don't like it."

"I hear you. And I am being careful."

As I said that, I dared a glance back in the kitchen. Mayzie was squealing and clapping her hands as Jax played airplane with her.

He wasn't one of the bad guys, was he?

Unfortunately, while I watched them play, I wanted to believe he was one of the good guys. But Adam had a point. Maybe it was time I stopped trusting people so blindly. "Okay, I promise I'm being careful. Please let me know as soon as you have anything on that ledger. Let's start getting our lives back, yeah?"

"You got it."

Bex hopped back on the phone. "Unlike Adam, I don't think bodyguard hottie is the bad guy. But I do think he's dangerous for your heart, so no matter what, watch your back, yeah?"

"Yes, thank you all very much. But I will remind you both that I do not need a mom."

I heard Adam grumbling something back. I ignored him and hung up. I might not like the fact that they were all over my business, but they did have a good point. Friend or foe, Jax Reynolds was dangerous, and I for one had no intention of getting hurt again.

Jax...

BY DAY two in the safe house, we were ready to kill each other. It was a tight space, and it was hot. It was always warm in the islands, but the heat wave had temperatures nearing the hundreds. Mayzie was uncomfortable. I was uncomfortable. And every time I could see the shiny sweat on Neela's shoulders or breasts, I thought back to that night, and it would start all over again. The pounding in my blood, the desert in my mouth, the inability to swallow, wanting her, needing her.

And then realizing it wasn't ever going to happen again because she hated me.

For the second time that night, I woke up drenched in sweat, unable to sleep.

Oh, and also my damn dick was *still* hard. I'd taken care of that problem earlier. I thought if I could just take the edge off, I wouldn't walk around wanting her, needing her.

I could smell her damn shampoo everywhere throughout the house. I'd thought living with her at Willa's house was bad but living with her in the bungalow was worse. It was a more confined space. Every time she stepped out of her bathroom, her scent was all I could smell. I was losing my damn mind. I'd been living in a permanent state of semi-hardness since we'd moved in.

I glared at the ceiling, willing it to be at least close to five, so it would make sense to get up. I concentrated so hard with my brain, I thought I'd actually pulled it off. Then I rolled over to check the clock, and it was not 5:00. More like 1:30. "Fuck," I mumbled.

I couldn't get her out of my damn head, and it was becoming more of a problem.

Well, you're still not allowed to sleep with her.

It was more than that though. It was like she was this unseen itch. The more I tried to ignore it, the worse it got. And God help me if I did scratch that itch. It just itched more. Nothing I did made it go away.

Finally, I swept the sheets back from the bed. They were soaked through, so I needed to change them and grab a shower.

What were the chances I could start my damn day at two in the morning?

Slim to none.

Before I stepped into the bathroom, I quickly checked the security perimeter. All was good. There would be an unholy racket if it wasn't, but everything was fine.

Or relatively. I knew that something was up with Neela. She'd been on that Sat phone forever the day before. I was pretty sure she was working with her team, trying to decipher the ledger, but she wasn't saying a damn thing to me about it.

And I knew from what she'd said earlier that she had some work to do while we were here. But her phone conversation had seemed more intense than basic client stuff. I could tell it was getting to her that she didn't know how long we would be here, who was after her, or any of those vital and important things.

In the shower, I turned the water hot to ease the chill out of my bones. It seemed counterintuitive since I'd been so hot before, but my sweat had chilled me. My body remembered exactly what had woken me up.

The scent of her was all around the bathroom. Her honey and lime permeated everything. The shower was still damp, which meant she'd been in here recently. Had she showered before she'd gone to bed?

Sure enough, the shampoo bottle was slightly uncapped. I couldn't help but lean forward and take a sniff. *Mate, you've lost it.* And what do you know? Blood rushed through my dick.

As the water sluiced down my back, I dropped my forehead to the tile and muttered curses under my breath as I glared at my dick. "Mate, we have to get this shit under control." But he wasn't in any damn mood to listen

He knew what he wanted. *Her.*

"Well, think of something else because it's not happening."

I wrapped my hand around the base of my dick and gritted my teeth when it jerked in my palm. Christ, one whiff of that damn shampoo and I was half out of my mind with need.

As water rinsed over my body, I used a pump of that honey-citrus softness and smoothed it over the length of my erection. I raised an arm on the shower wall, my body shaking with desire.

I had this under control. I smoothed it slowly at first, from a down stroke to a softer one up, rubbing my palm over the sensitive head, then back down on repeat. Over and over, thinking of her gloved tight around me, squeezing me with her inner walls, making my head explode.

The rush of electric acceleration ran down my spine, and my knees buckled. Fuck me. I coughed a curse. Legs too weak to hold me, arms certainly too weak to keep my face off the tile.

Neela Wellbrook was going to be the end of me.

Once I finally got my legs back under myself, I turned the water to frigid and forced myself to stay in the spray several seconds longer than I thought I could handle.

When I finally turned off the water, I dragged in a deep breath. We needed to accelerate this plan. Either have Bipps pay for a round-the-clock armed guard in one of those safe smart houses or apply more pressure to our most likely suspects. We needed to find out the threat to Neela and Mayzie's safety, or I wasn't going to make it.

I still didn't bother with the light. What was the point? Instead, I grabbed a towel and wrapped it around my waist and quickly got out. I was going to find a way to deal with this. I'd made the choice of coming to stay with her instead of Trace. I needed to live with my choice.

Yeah, because you overestimated your ability to keep your thoughts to yourself.

The crazy thing for me was that considering how long I'd been with my ex, I hadn't thought of her nearly as often as I thought of Neela, the woman I'd known for barely a month.

That's because you're obsessed with her.

Was I? Hadn't needing her gotten me into a lot of trouble? I needed to see her for who she really was. Dangerous. The problem with that was the more I saw, the more I liked.

It took me a couple of towels to make my hair dry and then I brushed my teeth again. I don't know why, but the action was automatic. I finished brushing, and just as I was sliding my toothbrush into its holder, I saw the handle of the door turning, and I froze.

When it pushed open, a sleepy Neela shuffled in, eyes half closed, heading straight for me.

I held my breath, unable to move and not sure what to say. Then she reached up. Instead of hitting the medicine cabinet, her finger dusted over my pecs. With a squeak, she snatched her hand back, and her eyes bolted open. "Oh my God."

"Relax, it's just me."

She blinked her eyes. "Jax? What the hell are you doing in the bathroom?"

"Well, it's a bathroom, so a couple of guesses there."

"Why are you in here so late?"

"I just had a shower."

All traces of sleepiness were gone now. Her hot gaze pinned to my pecs and roamed down. "I—wh—what are you—?"

I gritted my teeth and tried to refrain from saying some dumb shit like, 'Hey, beautiful, my eyes are up here.'

Yeah, I was an idiot. I liked that she was looking at me, but if she kept that up, I was going to have another erection. And I was pretty sure she would not appreciate that.

"Sorry, I didn't know you were in here. I just woke up sweaty, and I had a headache, so I thought would just get um—what is it called—"

"An ibuprofen?"

She nodded slowly. "Yeah. One of those." Her eyes drifted back to my chest.

A warm flush of pride crept through my chest as her face reddened. "Is there something you need, Neela?" My voice had automatically lowered an octave.

She licked her lips then, still staring at me like I was a steak and she had been starving for weeks. "No, I—I'm just going to go back to bed."

But she didn't move. She didn't budge. Instead, I shifted around her. "No, I'll go. You probably needed the bathroom, so I'll just—"

I tried to shift around her, but she was still staring at me, lips parted, eyes drinking me in, hands twitching. Rubbing up against her was inevitable and unavoidable. I knew she could feel every inch of me.

All.

Nine.

Of.

Them.

To distract her, I blurted out, "I um—I used some of your shampoo." God that was dumb. If she asked me what for, I'd need to lie convincingly.

She nodded absently as her gaze stayed on my chest. "Oh, okay. Why couldn't you sleep?"

I could lie and tell her I was too hot. Although that was only part of the truth. But then I told her the whole truth because I was tired of lying to her, to everyone, to myself.

"I was dreaming of you."

EIGHT

NEELA...

My dream was awesome. I couldn't even begin to explain how awesome on the scale of awesomeness. Jax was with me. As he was in most of my dreams the last few weeks.

And he was doing the most delicious things with his mouth and his fingers, and I was flying. His hard length was pressed up against me, insistent. His fingers were playing adeptly over my clit, and his hot mouth was pressed against my breast, sucking me deep. And around deep pulls, he murmured how beautiful I was, how he couldn't get enough.

But then, as the ecstasy started to spread through my body, the euphoria coming for me, there was an earthquake. We were shaking. Shaking him lose from my breast, prying his fingers from me, and I held on as tightly as I could. "No, Jax, don't stop."

The shaking stopped for a moment. But something had broken the magic. He had stopped sucking on me. He'd stopped driving me toward orgasm. And he was watching me, carefully. His mouth was moving as if he was trying to tell me something. But I couldn't hear the words, and the shaking started again.

Earthquake.

And then suddenly, I was yanked out of the dream, away from his hot embrace into the cold, harshness of the night. "Oh my God, what?"

Jax was there in person. "Wake up, it's time to go."

"What's happening?" That was a dream? Oh my God, it had felt so real.

His intense blue stare was on me again as if he wanted to ask me something, but he shook his head. "We don't have time for that. Shoes, jacket, now, baby. Go time."

I knew exactly what go-time meant. It meant, 'Come the fuck with me, ask no questions, and I'll keep you alive.'

I jumped out of the bed, the sheet tangling around me, trying to keep me where I was, as if it too knew that I needed to finish that dream. But there would be no finishing that dream tonight. Real Jax was making me do things. Real Jax was making me run, *again*.

He'd already gotten me in the habit of putting everything away in our go bags before we went to sleep. So it was just a matter of grabbing Mayzie in her sleep sack, putting my backpack on, sliding my shoes on and grabbing a jacket. Never mind that I was in a t-shirt and boyshorts, not perfectly proper attire. Not that I gave a fuck. If he was saying go time, it meant danger.

"Come on."

He had Mayzie's other bag and his one bag. He also had a weapon.

Just seeing him hold a gun and how he handled it almost like a lover, I wondered how in the world I could have ever thought he was a manny. He was so at home with the gun.

He pressed his fingers to his mouth and held up a tablet, showing me movement on the south room wall. Someone was inside our goddamn safehouse.

I blinked rapidly and then nodded, praying that Mayzie stayed asleep. I grabbed the baby carrier and rapidly latched her in, praying to God I could move quickly enough.

Jax wasted no time. When we were at the back door, he held up his night vision goggles, and I could almost see the tension rolling up his shoulders as if he was relaxing. "We've got a clear path. See those trees over there, almost intersecting at the corner of the gate?"

I nodded. "Yeah."

"That's where we're going."

"Are we going over the gate?"

He shook his head. "No, we're going through. You hit the right place and that opens right up. There's a secondary car well off the path through the backwoods for half a mile. There is a car waiting there for us, okay?"

I frowned. "But we have a car."

He sighed. "We have to go through there to get it." He pointed the direction of the garage. And since the garage was not connected, we'd be open as we ran to it. "Oh, lead the way. I got this."

"Are you sure you don't want me to carry her?"

"Nope, let's go."

He was right. We were in danger, and I was asking questions. Dumb. So dumb. I could ask all the questions in the world wherever we wound up. With a deep breath, he was out the door, gun at the ready.

But then there was a series of beeps from his watch, and he cursed. “Change of plan. Go back in the bedroom, through the bathroom, and into the second bedroom. If I'm not in there in three minutes, climb out the window, head for the west corner of the gate, and then head for the shore. Use the sat phone to call for help."

"What? I—"

But he shoved me toward the bedroom and flipped the safety off his gun.

He really would protect us with his life.

It was still the last thing I wanted. What I wanted was my old life back. Simple. Uncomplicated. Where people weren't trying to kill me every minute.

Except, I wanted that life with Mayzie in it. We'd had a rough start, but after a month, I didn't understand how she hadn't been mine all along.

You have Jax to thank for that.

I did have him to thank. He might be a liar, but he was great with Mayzie. Better than great. I probably wouldn't have survived this long without him.

Mayzie was sleeping like the dead in her little sleep sack. I grabbed the bag he'd dropped and slung it over my shoulder, cross-body style, and ran back into the bedroom with her.

I needed a weapon. Something. What if Jax didn't catch the intruder?

There was an umbrella hanging behind the door.

Praying that Mayzie kept silent, I crept back into the room, tiptoed over to the door as quietly and gently as I could, and slid it off the hook. It would have been a lot easier if I didn't have to hold the baby.

I eyed the bed sheet. That might be too big. Then I remembered the cot in Mayzie's room with a twin sized mattress. And there were sheets to fit it in the closet.

Carrying the baby, the umbrella, diaper bag, and my go bag, I ran back to the room and grabbed the sheet that I would need.

I eased her back into the crib gently, put the bag and my makeshift weapon down, and set it all up.

Once I had Mayzie strapped to my back, many thanks to my improvised bed sheet, I grabbed the cross body and my umbrella weapon, then went back to the door.

At the door to the living room, I listened closely. When I heard tussling and grunting, I dared to ease it open and peeked around.

Jax was fighting with someone.

Someone smaller.

I knew it was stupid. I knew it was dumb. But still, I ran into the fray as if I could do anything to save Jax. He was basically every action movie star I'd ever seen in my life. And he looked like he was trying not to kill the person in his arms.

He grunted. "Stop fighting. I won't kill you if you stop fighting." Then there was a slice. Something glinted in the moonlight and I screamed out. "Knife."

They both turned. Unfortunately, Jax was focused on me, and the smaller intruder almost got a piece of him. He jumped back just in time, but it gave the intruder the opportunity to pull a gun.

I didn't even think. I just ran out with my umbrella raised high, ready to strike, aiming for the intruder's arm.

It was only when I was within a step that a trick of the light stopped me. "Willa?" No. I shook my head. Willa was dead.

I froze.

Jax had his gun back in his palm. "You two know each other?"

I stared at the intruder, mouth agape, praying that Mayzie was still asleep.

She wasn't making a sound on my back, but that didn'tmean anything because I wanted to shield her from this if I could.

My dead best friend grinned at me. "Neela, oh my God. I'm so glad I found you."

"You're not dead?"

"Rumors of my death have been greatly exaggerated."

Another beep of the alarm sounded on his watch, and Jax cursed and glared at her. "You bring some friends?"

Willa shook her head. "No. but there are people after me. And—"

He shook his head. "We don't have time for this. Let's move." To Willa, he said, "Come with us or stay. I don't care either way."

Shell-shocked, I followed him. My mind teetered around like a drunken sorority girl as it tried to make sense of what was happening. Mayzie snuffled on my back. Quickly, I modified the makeshift sling so she sat against my chest, then I pressed her head against me and did as I was told.

Luckily, she'd slept through our little adventure so far. She was too busy sucking her thumb, and given the way she was twitching, she was having her own little baby dreams.

Outside, the grass felt cool as it tickled my ankles. It was a bit longer than when we got there, probably thanks to the rain for the last few weeks. We took so little with us when we ran. I was sad looking back at the house. I'd gotten used to it. Maybe it hadn't been home, but at least it has been somewhere safe to lay our heads for a few days. Now I was already missing it.

Behind us, I heard movement. I didn't dare turn around. I just kept crouched, marching behind Jax. Willa was to my side. Suddenly, he stopped then jumped behind me and Willa. He began walking backward, watching our backs. "Keep moving to the gate." His voice was a harsh command.

I heard a twig again, and this time he fired his gun without hesitation. I watched, stunned as he fired, but there was barely a sound. Only a small *pfft*.

"Keep moving."

My heart hammered in my chest. The sweat was already forming on my brows, but I did as I was told. I had to get Mayzie to safety, then I could freak out and pay attention to the sticky sweat that I could taste at the back of my throat, the swimming in my head, and the shaking hands.

I was going to focus on getting Mayzie the hell out of there, and then I would freak out.

I reached the gate and shoved until it opened. Willa went through first. I followed with Mayzie, and Jax was behind me. We shimmied through the opening and then closed the gate.

"Run!" Jax said in a commanding voice.

He had his flashlight out and showed me the path. "Come on, let's go." He took my hand and dragged me behind him. There was no careful, quiet track now. This was a full-on run for our lives. And boy did I run. Everything felt slower because I had Mayzie strapped to my chest and my pack on my back, but I did my best to keep up. And Jax didn't let us fall far behind. There were times where I felt like he was literally dragging me off my feet behind him. It was the longest half-mile I'd ever run in my life. When we reached the car, it looked like some muscle car. I didn't know what it was exactly, but I thought it was a Dodge. I recognized the emblem.

He dragged the tarp off of it and unlocked my side. "You're going to have to hold her. There is no car seat. I'll solve that later."

I nodded numbly and unstrapped her from my body. Then I climbed in, put her on my lap and tugged the seatbelt over us.

Jax jumped into the driver's seat, started the car, and gunned the engine. Willa was crouched in the back, watching the woods as if she was waiting for the boogeyman.

Jax hit the gas, and we started to roll at an alarming speed. And just in time, because someone ran through where we'd just come from, emerging from the blackness that was the forest.

But Jax was screeching out of there. As soon as we came out of the woods, we locked onto a road and headed east.

It wasn't until we'd been driving a good five minutes at a breakneck speed that I started to breathe again, unaware that I'd been holding my breath the whole time. "Who the hell were those guys?"

"I don't know. But the safehouse was compromised. We'll have to take our chances at a hotel."

"Oh, okay. Whatever you say."

He slid me a glance and then a wry smirk. "I feel like this is the first time you have ever uttered such a phrase in your entire life."

"You wouldn't be wrong."

He flicked his gaze to Willa. "Don't think you're getting out of this. You have a lot of explaining to do."

Jax...

WHAT IN THE name of Jesus, Mary, and Joseph was going on? Willa freaking MacKenzie was in the back of the car. Alive. And from the looks of it she wasn't a reanimated zombie.

She'd also brought armed heat on her tail.

She kept looking behind us. But I had to wonder if it was real fear or contrived?

I drove them to the next ferry landing, then we hopped another ferry to Lords Island. Only then did I think it was safe enough to stop. How was it that I was on plan B already?

Something had gone very fucking wrong. How the fuck had Willa MacKenzie known how to find us? And who were those armed men? Had they been following her, or were they fucking independents?

I had to resist the urge to shake her and demand answers. Safety first. Neela and Mayzie were my priorities. Once the ferry landed us on Lords Island, I reached into Neela's go bag and pulled out some clothes. Then I turned to Willa. "Strip."

Her eyes went wide. There was something I couldn't read in them. Was it fear? Disdain? Lust? "You're kidding."

"Jax. What the hell?" Neela's gaze was ping-ponging our exchange.

"She turns up out of the blue with arseholes with guns on her tail. So we're going to need answers, like who were they and how did they follow her. Maybe she's for real and she really did run for her life. I'm not taking chances either way that she has a tracker on."

Willa didn't move.

Then I pulled out my gun. "You can strip and hand over your phone and jewelry, or I can shoot you. Either way, my problem is solved."

Neela's gasp was soft, but it felt like I had swallowed needles. I didn't want to hurt Willa, but I would do anything necessary to protect Neela and Mayzie.

Willa put her hands up. "Okay. Okay. Relax." She handed me her phone.

I tossed it onto the ground then crushed it under my boot.

"Clothes. Now."

She stripped and changed in record time. Then I tossed all her possessions into the water and we got back in the car. "Happy?" She glowered at me.

"Immensely." I didn't give two fucks about Willa. Neela was my concern. She was quiet, and her breathing was shallow. Mayzie had begun to stir, and Neela's hands had been trembling when she patted her back to quiet her.

There was nothing but silence on the way to the hotel. Neela was likely having an acute anxiety attack. Willa, I couldn't make out.

Worse, I needed to check in. I wasn't the only one who'd gotten the perimeter breach alerts. When we stopped I'd check in. But I wouldn't be telling them where we were.

I trusted my team. I did. But we had a leak somewhere. Maybe an unintentional one, but still. Willa had known exactly where to find us. So had the armed goons.

I certainly wasn't using another safe house again. That way, if the leak was internal, nobody would know where we were.

When we reached the hotel, I took Willa with me to check in. That way I knew she couldn't alert anyone to our location. Instead of using cards, I paid with cash.

I was able to secure us a suite with three bedrooms. I'd roll the cot into the smallest room for Mayzie. It was more expensive, and we'd only be able to stay there for a week, maybe two, but I hoped that everything would resolve by then, and I'd slap Ariel with a fat-ass expense report.

As soon as we were in the suite, Willa reached to take

Mayzie from Neela, but I stepped between them. "Oh no you don't. We're going to talk, but not now. Neela has had enough, and Mayzie needs to sleep. First thing in the morning we're getting the whole story of your bloody resurrection."

"But I just want to hold my baby."

The hell I was going to let that happen. "And you will. After I ascertain the truth. It's three o'clock in the morning, so we'll all get some shut eye. Then we'll talk."

"Who the fuck died and put you in charge?"

"You actually. Now, that's you over there. I'll be on watch, so don't get any funny ideas."

Willa tried to look around me to Neela, but I blocked her path. "You don't look at her. You look at me."

She rolled her eyes and held up her hands. "Fine. You're in charge, big man."

With Willa in her room and Mayzie in hers, I ran my security protocols, getting cameras up and sensors on the windows. In the morning, I'd tap into the security feed using the black box Ariel had given me.

Neela came out of Mayzie's room. "Are you okay?"

Her question was soft, timid, as if she was afraid to talk to me. "Yeah, I'm fine. How's Mayzie? And how are you? You should be resting." I stood to try and corral her back to the bedroom.

"Mayzie's fine. You know babies, she slept through the whole thing. She'll wake up in the next town and have no idea what even happened."

"Kids are resilient. They bounce. I promise."

"Yeah, but how high a bounce?"

"You're still freaked out?"

She nodded solemnly. "I should be happy that Willa is back,

but instead, I'm scared. Terrified, actually. I've never seen anything like that. Do you—Do you think those men are gone?"

Of all the questions I thought she'd ask, that was probably not at the top of the list. "I don't know. Maybe. I don't usually go for kill shots unless I'm fired at first. But they had a chance and they didn't take it."

"Good."

My brows lifted. "Are you okay? You look a little shell-shocked."

She shook her head. "I don't know. I knew that Mayzie was in danger. Possibly me too. And then Willa walked in. My brain couldn't compute. Next thing I knew, men were shooting. Real guns. For what?"

"Very likely the ledger or money, but they won't find either one. You know I'm not going to let anything happen to you, right?"

She nodded. "I know. I just—"

I closed the laptop and stood. I slowly approached her and held out my hand. "Come here."

She stared at my hand for a long moment and then stood as well, placing her hand in mine. "Look at me. I want to check your pulse and make sure you're not in shock. Just keep talking to me."

"It's weird that I have nothing to say. I'm just— How do you do it?"

"It's a lot of training. The alarms went off, which is the reason you happen to be here in this place."

"I'm so scared. I had Mayzie in my arms and... I was just so scared."

I knew I shouldn't. I knew I was asking for trouble. I knew touching her again was going to mess with my head. But I couldn't watch her like this and not do something to help. I pulled her in close, and wrapped my arms around her, placing my chin on her head. "I promise you, you'll be okay. Take a nice deep breath. You're fine. I have you."

After several minutes, I could see the tension ease off of her shoulders. "You saved our lives."

"I certainly hope so. That is the job description."

"All this time I've been so caught up. I just—"

"This is a perfectly normal reaction. Don't be mad at yourself."

"I just don't know what to do."

I held her until more tension eased off of her. She pulled back and blinked up at me. "Thank you."

"You don't need to thank me."

Her gaze darted to my lips, and my body tightened. I knew she was still mad. I knew there was no way in hell she wanted me. And whatever the hell dream she'd been having before we made our escape, it was long gone, if she even remembered it. That didn't stop me though. As her gaze pinned on my lips and hers parted in a request, I knew I was going to lose my mind.

I watched her mouth as she nibbled the corner, like she did when she was nervous. Full and ripe, her lips invited me to taste them. Rolling my shoulders to loosen the tension, I closed the gap between us. I could ask for forgiveness later, but now, all I wanted to do was taste her again.

Before I dipped my head, I flexed and unflexed the hand at her waist, giving her a moment to walk away. But she didn't. Her lips parted, and the tip of her delicate pink tongue peeked out, moistening her bottom lip.

Body tense, I reached for her, massaging the back of her neck and her waist. "Neela." We stood like that for several moments as I worked the tension out of the back of her neck. I reveled in the feel of her delicate skin beneath my hands.

In the instant before our lips met, our breath commingled, and I could feel the energy ebbing from her. What was meant to be a soft, testing kiss, immediately changed to a more urgent one the moment her tongue met with mine

My blood ran thick and hot. The roaring in my skull a primal scream of need and desire. I deepened the kiss. Nella whimpered, her pliant body pressing into me, and I shifted my hand from her waist to her arse, palming it and pressing her closer.

If I'd ever had any fucks, I'd lost them now. She was letting me kiss her, and I was going to make it the best I could.

I brought my hands up from her waist to cup her face. "Neela."

She mumbled something unintelligible into my mouth. I didn't want to stop. Couldn't think of a reason to stop, so I nipped her ripe lower lip.

She rewarded me with a moan and wiggle, effectively rubbing her belly along the length of me. My erection surged and struggled for freedom from the confines of my pants. Reflexively, my hand clenched in her hair. Instinct and need clouded every rational thought to take it slow.

She responded by raking a hand up from the base of my neck through my hair. The action sent sharp tingles to each of my nerves. Straining for control, I ripped my lips from hers, using the hand tangled in her hair to hold her motionless.

I tightened my grip in her hair as my dick threatened to explode. "Do. Not. Move."

Her own harsh breaths mingled with her husky words as her heavy, lust-lidded eyes fluttered open. "I'm s—sorry, I—"

"Shh. Trying—get—control." My inability to form cohesive sentences surprised me. I'd been with plenty of women, but none of them ever made me feel like I had an electric current connected to my dick. I dragged in another breath.

"Why?"

More throbbing. My damn dick was going to all off. "Damn it, Neela—"

She silenced me by licking my bottom lip before she suckled it. My reaction was instant. In a swift movement, both hands scooped down over her arse, cupping it and then picking her up.

I braced her against the wall, just like the first time we'd made love, and adjusted her position so that my cock was directly situated against her.

She tasted like vanilla and strawberries, a decadent treat. At first, her tongue was tentative, and then her arms looped around my neck hard. Then she attached herself to me, kissing me back with all the ferocity that I was kissing her. My hands slid into her hair and angled her head just the way I liked it, so I could dive in deep with my tongue. I wanted to taste her, make her feel better.

All of a sudden it was like the kingdom of Heaven hadn't been close to me, and the one I couldn't see clearly was right in front of my eyes, and she was meeting me slide for slide, stroke for stroke and she wanted me too.

But then, just as suddenly as she kissed me, she pressed her hands against my chest. She was pushing me back. I tore my lips from hers. "What?"

"Make love to me."

Hell, yes.

Fuck, no. Geeze.

"Neela, I want you more than I should. More than makes

any sense. But what you're asking for right now, it's not real. It's because you're scared. Something terrifying happened to you, and you don't know what to make of it. You want to feel alive right now because everything else is too scary. I want you more than I've ever wanted anything, but I can't."

She blinked at me thrice. "You're saying no?"

I cleared my throat and released her. "Believe me, it pains me more than it pains you. But not like this. I want you to want me because of *me*. Not because you want to feel alive and you're scared. If you're scared, I can help you. I can help you feel safer. But let's not do *this* because of that."

She sighed and leaned back. "Oh my God, what in the world did I just do?"

"Neela, wait."

But she was already running from me. Again.

NINE

NEELA...

I'D KISSED HIM. Like an idiot.

I'd been keyed up and raw and tired and—

And you wanted to climb that man like a tree.

Fine, yes. I'd wanted him. And he'd been there, holding me, wrapping me in the warm, safe cocoon of his arms.

So I'd kissed him. I shook my head still trying to get my brain around it. I was pissed at him. Hurt by him. So why the hell had I thought kissing his stupid soft mouth would fix anything?

I didn't know when I'd fallen asleep. I'd been wound so tight after that kiss.

Mayzie had woken up, and I'd finally managed to get her back to sleep. I knew I shouldn't have let her sleep in bed with me, but after our midnight run, I wanted her close.

I wanted to hold onto her until Willa claimed her again.

Jax was in the living room on the couch. He'd wanted to watch Willa's room, which was honestly ridiculous.

Except, how the hell had she found us? And where the hell had she been all month? I wanted to be happy to see her... I did.

Mayzie had her mom back. But this was Willa. The only way this ended was with me unhappy.

In the end I barely slept. I was up with the sun, and so it seemed were Mayzie and Jax.

My only warning was the soft knock before he barged into my room to get her when she woke. "You know, you're not actually her manny. You don't have to jump with every little cry. I can handle it."

He watched me warily. "I know. It's sort of a habit now. Besides, Mayzie May and I sort of have a short hand."

The door to the other room opened and I stiffened.

As usual, he took notice and knew just what I needed. "Why don't you grab a shower. I'll feed Mayzie. When you're feeling refreshed, you can tackle the other stuff."

Just when I wanted to keep hating him, he said something sweet.

After a shower, I stalked into the living room ready to face everything.

"Jesus Christ, Willa."

Her smile was saucy. Her hair was freshly washed, and she looked as beautiful as always. "In the flesh. So, I guess you want me to explain."

"Yeah, I mean, you're fucking alive. So maybe start there."

Jax scowled at Willa from the kitchen, holding Mayzie protectively.

"Jax, it's okay."

His gaze didn't even waver. "No, it is bloody well not. Until we get some explanations, nothing is okay. She shouldn't have known where we were. Therefore, she can't be trusted."

I swallowed hard. He had a point, but still. "She is Mayzie's mother. She wouldn't hurt her."

He lifted a brow, and I could almost see the cocky, sardonic grin that wanted to break out. "Yeah, so you're telling me you're okay with the zombie in the room?"

"Oh my God, zombies can't talk. Everyone knows that."

Willa was far less amused by our exchange. "You two done flirting now?" She slid him a glance, rolled her eyes, and then her gaze darted back to me. "Where did you pick him up from?"

"Well, your lawyer, Mr. Bipps, insisted that I needed security. He came with the package."

She nodded. "Yeah, I insisted on it."

"First of all, why? And second of all, thanks for not giving me any choice."

"Look, the people that were after me, I didn't know if they'd come after Mayzie. I had to protect her."

"Jax, give us a minute, please."

He scowled, but then took Mayzie and her cereal into her room.

Willa took that opportunity to slide her gaze all over him. "When I said security, I didn't know that they were going to be hot, or I would have hired them myself. Jesus."

I rolled my eyes. "He's all right if you like big and bossy."

"So, you and big-bad bodyguard?"

Oh no, I wasn't getting distracted. "None of your business."

She held up her hands. "Um, it's absolutely totally my business because he works out shirtless, so I'm well acquainted with exactly what you're working with. And I am not mad at you. Way to get you some. I'm glad my fake death got you laid."

"This is not about me. Can we talk about how you faked your own death?"

"I had to. There were some seriously dangerous people after me, and I'd gotten in way over my head. I never meant to involve you, but I knew that you were the only person on earth who would look after Mayzie properly."

"Maybe you should have told your mother that, because she's threatened to sue me for custody."

She sighed. "Ignore her. She wants money. Lots of it. I have a provision in my will if she does that."

"Willa, she didn't even know you were dead."

"Yeah, well, she wasn't supposed to know. It's not like we've talked in years."

"Well, you know, you and I haven't exactly talked in a long time either."

Willa sighed. "I'm sorry about that. Look, I had to cut you out. I knew you were right."

"Willa, you can't just turn back up and think everything is cool."

Willa eyed me up and down. "Explain to me why you're dressed and he's not? Because if I was in a room with that man and he was shirtless, I'd be naked, honey."

"Shut up."

She grinned at that. "You're not such a goody-goody anymore, are you?"

"Focus. Explain to me why the hell you faked your own death."

"Look, from the beginning, the gallery was a passion. I loved art, you know that. And things were going great. But I didn't have quite enough business acumen. I was never like you. The numbers, they just never made sense to me."

"You could have asked for help at any time."

"Yeah, but you know how it is. My stupid pride."

I crossed my arms, and Willa sat at the tiny dining room table. She eased into a chair and fingered the fake petals of the plant there. "Yeah, so there was this guy. He told me that he would pay me to, you know, to ship things and certain artifacts. The key was I couldn't ask questions. You know, I got some local artists to make these vases. I had a gallery opening for them. And you know how art is. People will pay anything. So, I upped the sticker price. And I made a hefty amount on top of my commission for shipping the item to the owner. So I would get paid by the buyer, and then get paid by the person who wanted their items moved.I was a great middle man. No one was supposed to get hurt. And I didn't know what was in the art at first. You have to believe me."

"But you knew the people you were working with were bad news."

Willa nodded. "Yeah, that's why I got out. I wanted a safe home for Mayzie. But people like that, they don't just let you out."

"Willa, why is it always something like this with you?"

"You don't understand. I really wanted to be free. When it was clear that they were never going to let me go, I built my insurance contingency."

"The ledger."

She nodded. "It belongs to Alex Vanhorn."

My jaw dropped. "I've seen the news Willa. He's seriously bad news. He's into everything from drugs to arms to human trafficking. I knew you sold some pieces to him, but you stole from him too?"

She didn't answer. "Let's just say I made some bad decisions. Either way. But if I can crack the code, I'll have proof of the kind of guy he is, and I can buy myself a little breathing room."

I stared at her. "So, you used me. You placed me right in the line of fire to save your own skin."

She frowned. "You're all I have. Don't you see that? You've always been all I had. My parents, as cold as they were to you, they were awful to me. I could only ever depend on you."

"Don't. What about your little girl? You placed *her* in danger. For what? Money? All that money in your accounts. Where did it come from?"

"Look, just because I played in the sand box with the wrong people doesn't mean it wasn't lucrative. But I'm trying to do better. *Be* better. *For* Mayzie. But the problem is you don't get out once you're in. You were all I had, my only chance."

"What about the police, Willa?"

She shook her head. "They would have sent me to jail. Why can't you see that?"

"So you chose to risk *my* life instead."

"No, I chose to *save* Mayzie's. I'm getting out. I just needed help to get there. I want to be the kind of mom Mayzie can be proud of."

"She doesn't need all that money, Willa. She just needs you."

Willa shook her head. "I know. I messed up."

"How did this even start?" Out of the corner of my eye, I saw Jax prowling the bedroom. I knew he was listening.

"When I first discovered the drugs and the diamonds in the pieces I was asked to move, I wanted a bigger cut. I had other vases shipped in their places, and then I asked for more money. One of the buyers refused to pay. Two shipments were supposed to be going to two different places. I held on to them. As collateral."

"Oh my God, you're insane."

"It wasn't supposed to end badly. But then I noticed there were men outside the gallery, sitting in a van, watching me. I could have sworn I was being followed home. That's when I started installing bullet proof glass everywhere. It cost a pretty penny, but I had to keep Mayzie safe."

"Still no police."

"Look, I know. I made bad choices. I know that now. But I realized they weren't going to stop. They wanted their shipments, and they just didn't know where I hid them. And I knew I had to keep Mayzie safe and vanish. I wish I could have thought of a different plan."

"Oh my God, so you used me. Just like always."

"This is different, okay? I'm in real trouble here, and I'm Mayzie's mom. You're my best friend. I need your help. Look, I got in trouble, okay? Michael Satorini, his father is the Italian billionaire. His mom comes from cartel money, rumored to anyway. He is completely untouchable. He and I, we had history. He—he's Mayzie's father. He didn't—I didn't tell him at first. But I asked for his help to get out. He helped me steal the ledger, but we had no one to read it. I just want out, Neela. I need help."

“I'm not sure what I can do.”

“Look, you have one cipher. But there was another one.”

I frowned. “What do you mean?” And then it stuck me. “How do you know we found the cipher?”

She shifted slightly. “I left it for you. I didn't want to give them to you together, in case Michael double crossed me.”

“Nice friends you have.”

“Believe me I know. The first cipher was at the gallery. But there is another one. The pages on the ledger at the end. I don't know if you noticed. There were a series of indents, symbols. They would have looked like they are part of the paper?"

My brows drew down as I tried to remember. "Yes. Maybe, but just on the later pages."

She nodded. "Yes. Those are another code."

My heart rate ticked up, the light injection of adrenaline making me come alive. "Are you sure?"

"I have another cipher. I stole it with Michael. And when I left, I took it with me."

"Jesus Christ, Willa."

"Look, I know. I was hoping you'd be able to read the journal and then when I came back I could add the missing piece. I didn't know all this would happen. But things with Michael became contentious, volatile. He grew more violent, and he never wanted any part of Mayzie. I knew I couldn't stay, but I knew he wouldn't let me go. We stole that ledger together but I couldn't let him keep it. Whatever was in it, he wanted access to it and his cut of the proceeds."

I was tired of being lied to. Tired of not knowing who to trust.

"Where is he now?"

She swallowed hard. "We, uh, had a little disagreement about Mayzie. He wanted to leave her behind. I didn't. He wasn't pleased about that decision. He refused to let me leave. Said he couldn't trust me."

Jesus. I had no idea what to believe. If she was telling the truth, then she was in the kind of danger I wouldn't wish on my worst enemy.

"How did you escape?"

She shrugged. "Took him to bed, drugged him, and strolled out the door. His men still thought we were partners."

"Let me guess. Those were the men at the safehouse?"

She nodded. "Maybe. I tried to take steps to avoid being followed. No way to be sure though. Right now, I have a lot of enemies."

I ran my hands through my hair and tried to take it all in. "But the car accident... How did you do it?"

"The car? It was rigged to drive off the road. I faked the tire tread and basically pushed the car off the road. There are no lights out there. At night, no one drives that stretch. It's too dangerous. And there are no guard rails. It was easy pushing the car off the edge. I had a driver pick me up and take me somewhere safe."

"But your blood, it was all over the car."

"I know. Remember I donate blood? Like my good deed?"

I nodded. "Yeah?"

"I had a bag of my own blood. I spread it all over the front seat so everybody would think I was dead, even though they'd never find my body."

"So you risked everything. Mayzie, me, my life, because of money?"

"No, not because of money. I had no choice. They were going to kill me. Kill Mayzie. And I couldn't let that happen."

I stood, wiping my clammy hands on my jeans. "One more question... How did you find us?"

I couldn't tell what it was that flickered in her gaze, but there had been something. "I followed you."

I blinked at her. "You followed us?"

She nodded slowly. "Yeah. The house security feeds, I heard everything about your locations, and I've been watching you since I died."

"That whole time you could have saved Mayzie the pain and you didn't?"

"I had no choice."

"I don't know, Willa. From where I'm sitting, there were a million other choices. The ones you made though, put everyone you claim to love in danger. And somehow I'm not surprised."

TEN

JAX...

I WATCHED Neela and Willa surreptitiously from the bedroom, Mayzie in my arms. Where had she come from and how had she found us? And what the fuck was she doing coming back?

It hadn't escaped my notice that Willa had barely asked about Mayzie. There was no emotional, tear-filled reunion with her baby. Just stone-cold wanting something from Neela. We'd all been wrong.

Bipps had been worried about kidnap and ransom, but this was about something more. Willa *needed* Neela for whatever stunt she'd pulled. And she was more than willing to put her own child in danger to get her help.

I already wasn't a fan.

But from the look on Neela's face, my opinion would not be welcome. She looked open and relieved and happy.

No way she was that naïve.

Yeah, but all you see is danger and shadows.

I slipped into the adjoining bathroom with the sat phone and called home base. Ariel answered right away. "What the fuck? Where are you?"

"Well, funny you should ask that. The safe house was compromised."

She muttered a curse. "Jesus Christ."

"We have a leaky boat."

There was a breath of silence. "It's not the team."

"I'm not going to argue with you about whether it's the team or not, or Bipps himself. Hell, it could even be Adam or Bex. But unwittingly, someone did something that pointed to our location. Either way, we have a leaky boat."

"Where are you now?"

I chuckled. "You see, the thing about the leaky boat is, once you plug it, the best way to keep it plugged it is to say nothing. We're safe. That's all you need to know."

"You don't even trust me?"

"Of course, I do. You need me. But right now, I can't trust anyone."

She understood what I was saying. There was no denying it. Clearly, there had been a problem.

"I assume you're on the move?"

"We've settled for the moment. But we have other problems."

"Christ. Are you ever going to call me when you have good news?"

"Well, this could be good news in a way."

"What?"

"Are you a true believer? Because you should be. Willa MacKenzie has come back to life."

"What the fuck?"

"You know, those were my sentiments exactly. First, she found us. Her explanation for it is weak. You need to sweep for bugs. She's been listening in on our conversations in the house.

She says that's how she found us."

Ariel's string of inventive curses was impressive. I knew she had it in her, but some of the stuff she said wasn't exactly anatomically possible. "What in the hell is going on?"

"Do a sweep. Do it now."

"Shit. I'm on it. So, are you gonna tell me where you are?"

"Nope. Right now, I'm trusting nobody. It's easier. Safer."

"I hear you. The clients are safe though?"

"Yeah, they're right as rain."

"Willa MacKenzie. Jesus. So, she's after the ledger then?"

"Ding, ding, ding. She rolled out some sob story, and I need to keep Neela from believing every word that comes out of Willa's mouth."

"She's buying it?"

Even though I couldn't see them anymore, I slid my glance in the direction of the living room. "Let's just put it this way, she *wants* to buy it. She wants to believe her."

"And you don't."

"Remember that thing I said earlier about trusting no one? Especially not motherfuckers who rise from the dead."

"Okay, keep a close eye on Neela then." There was a pause, and then she asked, "Did Willa even ask about Mayzie at all?"

"Nah. She didn't even seem to notice Mayzie was in the room for the most part."

"Mother of the year that one."

"Maybe she's under duress. I don't know. All I know is that I'm currently roommate with the enemy, and I need to get her as far away from Neela and Mayzie as possible."

"Are you sure you don't want back up?"

"Back up requires telling you where I am, and I'm not ready to do that yet. That ledger, it's safe, right?"

"Yeah, locked up tight somewhere no one else can find it. Why?"

"I think it's the key to all of this. Keep on alert."

"Okay. We'll be on alert. Check in tomorrow."

"Yeah, when it's safe." I hung up on Ariel and stared down at the phone. The possibilities were endless. Willa could have found us a dozen different ways and not a single one of those ways made me at all comfortable. It was plausible that she'd been listening in.

Either way it made me uncomfortable to have her right under my nose. Sure, I could watch her. But she could easily be working against me. As soon as I had a chance, I needed to separate her from Neela and Mayzie. Now, I just had to figure out a way to make Neela happy about it.

Neela...

"I DON'T TRUST HER." Jax's voice was low and deep, nearly a growl.

I knew exactly what he was asking. That niggling, whisper of doubt in the back of my mind wouldn't stop. But I didn't give an inch. "What?"

The breeze from the balcony felt cool on my skin.

Jax peered through the open balcony blinds. Willa was holding Mayzie, who was crying. I could tell that Jax wanted to run in there.

"Even Mayzie isn't buying it. She's not even doing the right move. You've got to do the bounce and pat."

I eyed him and lifted a brow. "Look, as sweet as I think it is that you know Mayzie so well, Willa is her *mom*."

"Her mum who faked her own death. She *left* her to you."

I knew what he was saying. All night I'd been up tossing and turning with what I knew to be true. "But look, she's back now, okay? There's not much I can do about it. I can't stop her from seeing her daughter. And hello, she's *not* dead."

"You're buying it? You're buying her cockamamie story?"

"You know, not everyone is as cynical as you, Jax."

"How did she even find us?"

"She explained that this morning. She's been listening at the house. She still has access to the security feeds."

Jax lifted a brow. "Oh really? And that doesn't bother you at all? That she's been watching you without your permission?"

I swallowed hard. It did bother me. My brain kept replaying what she'd seen. What she'd heard. "She was worried about Mayzie. Not everyone lies."

He winced but wasn't deterred. "She didn't want us to know. Neela, look, I get it. She's your friend. But think about it. Every action she has taken has landed her in this position. Landed *you* in this position. And Mayzie. I'd be really careful about trusting her, if I were you."

"What do you want me to do? All I can do is accept the fact that she has come back. She's Mayzie's mom."

"Bollocks. *You* are Mayzie's mum. When she was sick the other week, Willa wasn't there. *You* were. We were the one holding her, concerned about her. You were the one calling the doctor, getting her into a lukewarm bath. *You*."

"*You* were with me."

"Yes, I was. The point is *Willa* was not. She faked her own death to avoid criminals. Think about it. Her first move was not to call the police, but rather to fake her own death, abandon her child, and drag you into this mess."

How could he not see it was her only option? "She was in danger. She had to do what she did to protect herself."

"Which meant putting you in danger? I love how with all of this protection, none of it included actually calling the authorities."

I opened my mouth, but then I had to shut it quickly. He had a point.

"The point is we have to keep her safe. She's in real trouble."

"That's an excellent idea. Let's go to the police. Do you think Willa is going with us?"

"Keep your voice down."

Inside, Mayzie only screamed more.

Willa bounced her some more and tried to shush her. And finally, Willa just put her down in the play pen and then went and plopped herself on the couch and turned on the TV.

Jax pointed inside. "You see what I mean? She's not even that interested in the baby. *Her* baby that she supposedly came back for. She's not interested."

"She's frustrated, okay? Imagine you've gone away and come back and found that your child had a new family."

"A family she gave her. My directive is clear. Keep you safe. Keep Mayzie safe. Nothing else matters."

"Well nothing is black and white like that. You can't go your whole life thinking that way."

"I can't believe *you* said that." He stepped into my space.

I resisted the urge to back up and craned my neck up to blink at him. "What?"

"You. Everything has to be just so. And then the one time

where thinking in black and white would make a lot of sense, where it would actually save your ass, you can't bring yourself to pull it off."

"Look, I'm doing the best that I can here." I shoved down the instinct not to trust Willa. She was back for her daughter.

"She's back at a convenient time. Danger is all around. There is something she wants, and you have to recognize that. Wake up. She is not your mate."

"What happened to make you so fucking cold?" The words escaped and part of me wished I could recall them.

He flinched as if I'd hit him. "I'm not cold."

Well, in for a penny, in for a pound. "Maybe cold is the wrong word. But distant. There is something so remote about you. That part of you that can't see that this is a good thing. That this is good for Mayzie. *I* am not her mother."

He slapped a hand on the railing as he crowded me. "Well maybe you bloody should be."

It was my turn to flinch. That secret wish. The one inside when I watched Mayzie sleep. The one I held onto when she would give me her baby grin, full of all three toothlets, and she would excitedly talk to me as if she was saying something of vital importance. Could I give that up?

Was I supposed to? I had no idea what to do. I hadn't intentionally fallen for Mayzie. But one look at her, and I was lost. Was Jax right? Should *I* be her mother? Or was I supposed to be her auntie?

Her mother is back. You are no one's mother.

I swallowed hard against that truth. "No, I shouldn't be. Her mother is back, and now we have to deal with those consequences."

I rushed past him, leaving him behind on the balcony.

ELEVEN

JAX...

She couldn't see it.

I was willing to wager she'd been more of a mother to Mayzie in a month than Willa had ever been.

She was being stubborn about it. Why? Why wouldn't she see?

I followed her inside. Mayzie had already started to nod off back in the confines of her playpen. Willa just continued watching television. Mayzie would never sleep properly with the noise, so I picked her up and took her into the other bedroom before heading for Neela's room.

Willa didn't even blink. *Did you expect her to?*

I didn't bother knocking on the closed bedroom door but instead just barged in.

Neela scowled at me. "What the hell, Jax? I need a minute." She turned then, away from me.

Maybe if I was cool and rational she'd see sense. I'd lost my temper before. Also, I wanted to make it impossible for Willa to listen in. I knew for a fact the walls were thick in this hotel.

"I'm sorry. But right now, you and I are the only ones looking out for Mayzie, so we need to be on the same page."

She whirled around, and I could see the shimmer of tears in her eyes.

I was an arse. I'd made her cry. "Shit, Neela..."

"You think I don't feel it? Like she's mine? Of course I feel it." Her voice dropped to a harsh whisper. "All these feelings only to have Willa waltz back in here like my life hasn't changed forever."

Two strides and I had her in my arms. I cocooned her to me like I could keep the scary things away.

Lies. Because the truly scary thing was in the bloody living room at the moment. Didn't matter though. As long as she let me hold her, I could give her false comfort.

She held on to me tight, her softness pressed into me. "Why can't you be real? Why can't any of this be real instead of a nightmare? I'm awake and watching the things I want slowly being ripped away from me."

My hands shook. She was so soft. The scent of honey and lime wrapping around me as always. My voice was harsh when I said, "I'm very real. And I'm not going anywhere unless you tell me to go."

Her voice barely above a whisper, she said, "I don't want you to go."

My fingers glided over the small of her back in the barest hint of a caress. Electricity shot through my body like I'd been struck by bloody lightning. Or at the very least stuck my finger in a socket.

I only ever felt like this with her. Anyone that came before was a mere shadow in comparison.

"Jax..."

My name was a question. "Neela, if I touch you again, I'm not letting you go. I don't want to go back to pretending."

I willed the words I wanted to hear. At least it felt that way. "I know. I'm scared."

I could assure her that I'd keep her safe, but I knew what she was really saying. "Me too."

Neela stepped back and unzipped her skirt, easing it past her hips. I had to force myself to swallow around the desert in my mouth. *Fuck.*

She let the silk fall to the floor. A low hiss issued through my teeth.

"Are you going to help me with this top? I had a bitch of a time getting these two little hooks done."

I couldn't help the smile tugging at my lips. "Oh, you need my help, do you?"

"Yes. This is one of those times it's okay to boss me around."

My mouth opened, but no sound came out. I shut it. Opened it again in another attempt. Still no sound. *Third time's the charm.*

This time as I spoke, my voice was distorted. Low. Guttural. "You want me in charge, Neela?"

She stepped forward again, closing the gap between us. "Yes."

There was a low humming sound, like a purr. It took me a moment to realize I'd been the one making it. She wanted me bossy and in charge.

Fair enough. Like an animal let loose from my chain I lunged for her.

I moved quickly, and her breath chased out of her lungs in a rush, leaving her gasping.

When I deposited her on the bed, I muttered prayers of thanks. She was mine.

And I intended to do what I could to keep it that way.

Neela...

JAX LOOKED like he wanted to eat me.

That wouldn't be a bad thing. Remember the last time.

Heat suffused my skin when I thought about the last time his mouth was on me.

Jax's gaze tracked all over me, hungry, lingering on my breasts. Instead of starting with my breasts as I anticipated, his hands went to my hair.

I expected him to be firm, possessive, but he was so tender. Gently he massaged and stroked slow circles at my temples. "Neela, you are so bloody beautiful," he murmured.

His breath was a whisper with mine before his lips brushed over my mouth. His kiss was soft at first. Coaxing even. With one arm bracing the majority of his weight and the other scooping under me to adjust my position, he settled me at a better angle.

Hand still cupping my ass, he deepened the kiss, taking long drugging pulls at my lips and eliciting a moan out of me. He licked into my mouth, intoxicating me.

I arched my body under his and could feel the length of his erection nudging at my hip. Begging for attention.

When Jax trailed his lips along my jawline to my neck, his teeth grazed my skin, and I shivered.

My hands trailed up his back, and his muscles bunched and

flexed under my touch. I'd seen his muscles so many times. I'd fantasized about him, running my hands over his skin.

Jax was a veritable expert at taking his time, each kiss laying out a path of seduction and electricity hot enough to singe my nerve endings. He moved to my breasts, and I sucked in a breath of air and held it. His breath cooled my too-hot skin in some places and added to the overheating in others.

"Your tits are fucking perfection, you know that?"

He wasn't looking for answers. Instead he dipped his head to kiss the underside of my breast, and the breath I'd been holding came out in a rush.

Another kiss, this one lingering. I could feel his cock strain and throb as my body arched into the caress of his lips.

Bracketing my hips with his wide, strong hands, he held me in place as he dipped a tongue into my belly button. "Open, love."

My hips jerked up, and his fingers dug into them. I wanted to comply, but I was shaking too badly.

Jax's thumbs stroked that expanse of flesh between my belly button and my pubic bone. Even as he trailed kisses to follow his thumbs, he murmured words of adoration and lust.

When he moved his kisses lower, I wiggled my hips in anticipation.

"Have you forgotten how this works, angel? You part your thighs, and I will make you feel so good. I want to lick you everywhere. I miss your fucking taste. And there are things I want to do to your tits. But you're going to come for me first. Then I'm going to have my way with you. Am I clear?"

I didn't realize I'd whimpered until the soft sound pierced the air. His thumbs snuck under the tiny patch of sapphire blue satin. "Is it okay if I get rid of theses knickers?"

I nodded. Jax, wrapped his fingers around the flimsy fabric and tugged, the tearing sound filling the air. "I'll buy you a new pair."

My skin heated. His thumbs nudged my lips, and he hissed again. "Bloody hell, angel, you're so wet for me. Are you thinking about the last time I was inside you?" He stroked me again, this time circling a thumb over my clit.

I whispered, "Yes."

Stroke. Circle. "Are you thinking about that first night when I put my mouth here?"

An involuntary shiver wiggled up my spine. "Yes." Oh God, he was going to kill me.

Stroke. Circle. "Good. I want you thinking about that." While one thumb kept up the slow circular motions on my clit, he shifted his other hand to slide a finger into my heat. "Hm, so tight. So perfect."

I moaned in pleasure as I buried my head further into the pillow. Shit. He really knew how to touch a woman. I was going to melt.

Jax…

SHE TASTED SWEET. The first stroke of my tongue had me groaning. Neela was so fucking perfect. And she was mine.

She slid her hands into my hair and I relished the impatient tug. God, she was so sexy. I had all the time in the fucking world. And I intended to use it. Especially now that I had her on my tongue again. The possession roared through me. *Mine. Only mine.*

I glided my tongue over the center of her soft core again, pausing to run my tongue in a slow, languid circle over the tight bud of her clitoris. She hitched a breath, and I smiled. "You like that?"

Her answer was a moan, and as she pulled my head closer to her moist center, I knew I was on the right track. "Tell me how you like it, Neela. Harder?" I demonstrated, and she groaned. "Softer?" I showed her what I meant, and I could feel her legs quiver around me.

"Harder." She gasped, and I obliged. Then she let out a soft curse.

I could feel her impending orgasm before she called out my name. I felt the telltale quiver of her thighs and tasted her sweet nectar on my lips. Her hands tightened in my hair. The sharp sting of pain made me shiver with need. My cock throbbed painfully, but I mentally wrestled it for control. I would not rush this. I would not be in a hurry.

Neela was different. Special.

As I kissed the insides of her thighs, she went limp and I whispered into her skin. How beautiful she was, how soft. I knew she probably couldn't hear me, but it didn't matter. I wanted to say those things out loud.

She might have thought I was done, but I wasn't. I kept up with the teasing until I dragged a second orgasm from her before I lost the battle of wills with my throbbing cock and balls. I needed to get inside her. Needed to feel her tighten around me.

"Jax, please."

Lifting my head, I watched in satisfaction as Neela's hands knotted in the sheets, and she threw her head back, ecstasy etched onto her face like the most gorgeous artwork. I didn't give her time to come down from her orgasm—tossing my T-shirt over my head, I leveled myself over her diminutive form. "Neela, look at me."

Lazy eyes blinked up at me, and the moment her eyes focused, she smiled the sweetest smile.

Fuck, I loved her. I knew it. I dropped my forehead to hers, our gazes locked. I would never be the same. She'd ruined me for everyone else.

I shifted her under me, and cupping her ass, I couldn't help but give her a squeeze. God, she was so sexy.

Her eyes remained on mine as I slid in to the hilt, widening as I stretched her. The moment her eyes clouded, I stopped and gritted my teeth against my need. "Are you okay?"

Her eyes narrowed up at me then she took matters into her own hands. She slid her hands down my back and drew me in deeper.

"Jesus." The curse escaped my lips before I knew what was happening. She wiggled around underneath me, encasing me in her slick heat from base to tip. Her eyes fluttered closed in an expression of bliss.

That did it. Unable to control my hips, I withdrew the tiniest bit and reseated myself inside her with a groan. Lowering my head to hers, I hissed in a breath.

As I thrust, I could feel her nails scoring into my back. Demanding me to move faster, harder. When she called my name, I was having the best fantasy of my life.

I felt the tingle at the base of my spine, and I gritted out, "Whoa. Stop."

Neela immediately went still. Forcing myself to stop the thrusting was another matter. My brain gave the command, but my hips didn't obey. Eventually, I pulled her tightly to me and rolled us over, not breaking the contact. Gripping her hips as I pumped, I begged her, "Ride me."

As she did, those magnificent breasts of hers swayed, and I thought there wasn't any other place in my life I'd ever want to be.

"Oh. My. God," Neela whispered.

I held on as her orgasm rolled through her and milked me.

Grip. Release. Grip. Release. *God.* As the tingle in my spine rolled through my gut, I followed her shout with a guttural one of my own. "Fuck, Neela." The strength of my orgasm forced me up off the bed. I held on tight, my hands grasping her sweat-slickened back as I soared into firelight.

She collapsed on top of me. As my eyelids fought the battle to stay open, I held her tightly to me. *My Neela.*

TWELVE

NEELA...

"So, you and Mr. Bodyguard?"

My face flushed. "Um, what do you mean?" The window was open to the balcony. I knew Jax could hear us out there.

"Honey, don't act like I couldn't hear you two last night. I mean, that must have been some hot dirty sex because all I heard was furniture rolling around, shushing, and then groans. Like deep manly groans. Please tell me that was a make-up fuck."

"Oh my God, Willa."

"What? He's on the balcony working, okay? He can't hear me." She turned to face me, and my gaze flickered over to the balcony. Jax looked at me and grinned and then mouthed, *Oh I can hear you.*

I was going to kill him.

"So, tell me all the juicy details."

"It's not... I, um..." I swallowed hard. "He—Jax and I, uh—it wasn't supposed to happen. It just kind of did."

"That's the best kind of happening, honey. How the hell do you think I got Mayzie?"

I groaned. "Please. I don't want to know. I already know way too much about your life that could possibly get us all murdered in our sleep.

She waved a hand. "The point is, I understand passion. And you guys... hmm, it's like every room you're in, you're boning each other with your eyes. That's somehow even hotter."

"How does one even bone with their eyes?"

"It mostly looks like you guys want to eat each other, and anyone who gets in your way is going to be dead. I approve. He's better than Richard. Ugh, Richard. How I hated Richard."

I scrunched my nose. "Did everyone hate Richard and just not tell me?"

Willa nodded and plopped on the couch. "Yep. We all hated him. You know, I don't even like Bex, but honey bunch and I were on the same page. Could not stand him. I still don't know why you put up with him for so long."

"Well, having someone was better than having nothing."

"You deserve better. I, for one, am happy that you're getting boned the way you need to be boned. I mean, he is giving you orgasms, right? Because you walked out this morning like your legs didn't work right. And if he's working you over that good, it should come with lots of pleasure."

"Oh my God. What is wrong with you?"

"I'm just saying."

"It's none of your business."

"Okay, okay. Sorry."

Jax's gaze was on his laptop, but he grinned again. And I could see the way his tongue peeked out and licked his lower lips. Yes, the man was a master with his tongue and he was taunting me, which wasn't fair.

I would get into that later. Much later. Right now, I had to focus on Willa. "Yes, it's really none of your business."

"Hey, if my best friend is getting some, it is absolutely my business."

I ignored the comment where she called me her best friend, because clearly, she was ignoring the fact that we hadn't spoken in well over a year. I hadn'tbeen there to meet her daughter. The first time I'd ever seen Mayzie was just a few weeks ago. But we were going to ignore all that and pretend none of it had happened. "Jax is, um, exactly what I needed."

That earned another grin. "Fantastic. Because you went far too long without."

He nodded along.

Jackass.

"Well, that seems to have rectified itself, hasn't it?"

Willa leaned forward. "I mean like, what does he do, because the little whimpers and moans I heard... I eventually had to put my noise cancelling earphones on. With those eyes, that intense kind of focus, I assume the man was good with his mouth?"

"Willa, we are not having this conversation."

"Why not? Okay, so obviously, he's good with his tongue. His hands are enormous, so he better know how to use them, and given your uncomfortable stance there, shifting from foot to foot, the man can lay some pipe. I'm a fan. But I have got to know, is he an anal guy?"

My jaw dropped open. "Oh my God, Willa!"

I couldn't look up at him. I knew he was looking at me. My traitorous eyes darted to him quickly, and of course, he was nodding slowly. My whole body clenched. Oh my God, I was going to die. That was the only way any of this was going to happen. I was dying. I waited for the ground to open up and swallow me whole.

"We are not having this conversation."

Willa laughed. "Still a prude, I see."

I refused to look at Jax. No way, no how. "I am not. It's just none of your business."

She rolled her eyes. "Okay, if you say so, but you don't want to be that girl who loses a man just because she doesn't know her way around sex. The kind of guy Jax is, he's going to get bored if you don't mix it up."

I cringed inwardly. What I said was, "I'm good, Willa. I got this." But what I thought was, 'She's absolutely right.' Playing it too safe had cost me too many relationships in the past.

If I wanted to keep Jax, I was going to have to get a lot more creative. Plain old vanilla wasn't going to suffice.

Jax...

THAT NIGHT when Neela was in the shower, Willa came out of her room. My gaze flicked up, but I ignored her. What were the odds that she'd just go away?

"I know you don't like me. You don't have to pretend."

"Good, because I wasn't pretending."

"Look, I know me just turning up here is problematic, and because of me, we have people on the islands that are looking for Neela and Mayzie. I'm sorry about that."

"Congratulations, you learned a new word."

"You know, we don't have to be enemies."

She slid down onto the couch next to me, her wide dark eyes

attempting to pierce into my soul. The difference was, I knew what she was doing. And I had zero interest in taking the bait. "I know you think that you can maybe sweet talk your way out of this, that maybe you'll wake up tomorrow and Neela will believe everything that you say, but she won't because she already sees it. And she's not worried about herself, unlike you. She's worried about Mayzie."

"Mayzie, Mayzie, Mayzie. Jesus Christ, you would think she was yours."

"Well, we've been the ones looking after her for the last month or so. Where the hell have you been?"

"I already told you. I was running for my life."

"You're running from a situation that *you* created. So, where does that leave Neela and Mayzie then?"

"I don't know. I guess I didn't think it through, okay?" She shook her head. "That's not why I'm even out here. I've been noticing you, the way you watch me."

"Well, I watch all potential enemies the same way."

"No, Jax. There's been something in your guise."

The hairs at the back of my neck stood at attention. "Oh, yeah? What's that?"

"Well, for starters, I couldn't have picked a better person as a bodyguard. I mean, what a stroke of luck."

Yeah, those hairs, *still* at attention. I scooted closer to the edge of the couch and placed my laptop down to turn to stare at her. "Just what the fuck is it you think you're saying? Get to it, because I have work to do."

"What the fuck I'm saying is, I'm better in bed."

That, I didn't expect. "What?"

"Look, I love Neela. I do. I just, I can feel that tension and vibe between us, you know? I feel it, and I know you do."

Oh, I felt something all right. Unfortunately, it was in the line of disgust. "You're off your rocker."

"I'm not. You have been watching me. And that intensity, God, no wonder Neela wants to keep you to herself. But, I mean, she told you, right?"

I lifted a brow. "What? What was she supposed to tell me?"

"Well, we pretty much shared every boyfriend since we were kids."

My stomach turned. The bile rose up in my throat, and then I knew what this was. "Is that so?"

Willa scooted closer. "Yeah. Usually, I get them first. Sometimes, they're Neela's first. You know, we're close as sisters."

"Oh yeah? Is that so?" I left out the fact that I had met her mother and had seen how her mother had treated Neela. There was nothing sisterly about any of this. Whatever fucked-up sisterhood thing Willa thought she had with Neela, it only served her.

"So what is it that you think you want from me?"

"Well," she lowered her voice. She pushed herself up to her knees and then straddled me on the lap. My automatic response was to go perfectly still. This was enemy territory. Any sudden movements could get my throat sliced. "I think that maybe while Neela is occupied, you and I can be occupied."

I met her gaze, searching it, trying to understand if this was a mirage, or if she was high or something. Her being high would certainly explain the behavior, but it was nothing like that. As far as I could tell, Willa MacKenzie was in complete possession of her faculties, which meant she was doing it just for fun.

I planted my hands on her biceps, and then I gently removed her off my lap and stood as she said, "What the hell?"

"Let me be clear with you, Willa. I am not interested in

fucking you. Not even a little. At all. If I saw you walking down the street, I would cross to the other side. You would not be someone that would ever entertain my interest. Am I clear?"

Her brows lifted and slowly descended as her lips flattened to a line. "Are you fucking serious right now?"

"Yeah, I am."

"You're such a dick. That's not even what I was saying. This was just a test."

"Does that work for you all the time? Pretending to test people in Neela's life when *you* are what's wrong with Neela's life?"

"I'm not what's wrong with her. You're the fucking *bodyguard*. It's not like she can actually be with you."

"Whatever Neela and I have going on is none of your damn business. Whatever little game you think you're playing won't work. I don't trust you. And, newsflash, neither does Neela, so stop with the fucking game playing, or you are going to get hurt."

The door to the bedroom opened and out came Neela in a robe. She took one look at Willa and I pressed together, and she raised a brow. "Just what the fuck is going on here?"

THIRTEEN

KING SEBASTIAN...

"Are you sure this is a good idea?"

I grinned at Roone. "Don't tell me you're chickening out?"

"Oh, I chicken out of nothing. But still, you really want to taunt the bull?"

I could read through his bullshit. He was worried and, so was I. This could backfire. "I thought you liked shaking things up?"

He rolled his eyes. "You're confusing me with your brother. Lucas is the one who likes to shake things up. I like rules. Rules are there for a reason."

I waved my hand. "Ah, don't be an old lady."

"Mate, my only goal in life is to protect you. You're sure they're not going to lose their shit?"

"If they do, it's not your problem."

"Until they try and have me killed."

"Well, it's a good thing you're a Royal Guard and a Knight."

He grinned then. "God, I fucking love that. Where's my sword, though? I really wanted a sword. And a shield."

"Jesus Christ. You and Penny with the round table thing."

"How are you a king and didn't love King Arthur and the Knights of the Round Table?"

"I mean, I liked it fine. But I don't have the level of obsession you and Penny do, apparently."

"Jesus Christ, you are an *actual* king and you've never had a round table of knights."

"Well, no. But now I have one. Happy?"

Roone rolled his eyes as he nodded. "Yeah. As long as I can take part in it."

"Show time." With a deep breath, I shoved opened the doors to the Regents Council Room. Despite all our efforts to modernize, there was always something dank about the room. The smell might be baked into the walls at this point.

The Council Room was located in the bowels of the castle. Deep underground, it had been created in King Jackson's time. It was meant as a safe location with enough hidden exits to the shore and to the city. The doors were also sealable in case of inevitable attacks.

Sir Gerald Lews approached us immediately. "Your Majesty." He bowed slightly. "Was there an agenda item I missed? Is there a reason Mr. Ainsley is joining us?"

I turned and grinned at Roone. "No. No agenda item you missed." The Council wasn't up for a vote until the next session. That was usually when we heard any testimony. And that was usually the only reason outsiders were invited to Council meetings.

Ethan had warned me about this. He hadn't exactly been against me creating Knights. He'd just been against me breaking it to the Council in this fashion. He knew they'd have something to say, but when done like this, I made it seem like I was performing a coup.

That's because you are.

"Let's get started gentlemen."

I liked Lews. He was our acting secretary. Smart. Measured. He usually voted with me, unless he felt strongly against something. But generally, he was a good guy.

When the meeting started, there were lots of raised eyebrows and murmured whispers. Everyone was wondering what Roone was doing there.

For his part, my best mate stood at my left shoulder. I was right-handed, and he was more than a little experienced in walking with me due to my time in the military. Since last year, Roone and I had worked on a shorthand. He always stood on my weak side, and he did what he had to do to guard me.

Most of the meeting went as planned. But every time someone had to speak on something mildly sensitive, their gazes all skittered to Roone.

As was standard, anyone who was there, even to give testimony, all signed an affidavit of complete silence. So they should have known Roone was safe, but still, they were uncomfortable. Across the table, I watched as Ethan shook his head. I could tell he was trying to hide a smile. His lips were twitching.

Finally, Ronald Coach cleared his throat. "Begging your pardon, Your Majesty, but this is highly unusual. Why is there a member of your Royal Guard here?"

I grinned at him. "I'm so glad you asked."

Everyone sat at attention then. "As all of you know, Roone Ainsley has been my right-hand guard for several years. He's a member of the Intelligence Team, highly skilled, responsible for bringing my sister home, and he's also her fiancé, as well as an Earl. As you're aware, during the next vote, we have seats up for election. You've also already been informed that I've put in Lord Ainsley's name for vetting and consideration."

There were murmurs.

Coach spoke again. "Yes, Your Majesty, we're all aware, but this is highly unusual. Why is he here now?"

"Well, if you wouldn't interrupt, you'd find out." I gave him a tight smile. "Lord Ainsley is also a King's Knight."

There was dead silence. Not a word was spoken. No pins dropping, not a mouse skittering. The silence had the full catastrophic weight of an explosion.

Finally, Coach sputtered, "A King's Knight? But there haven't been King's Knights for generations now."

"No, there haven't been. The King's Knights were merged with the Royal Guard, as you all know. And the Council, as a whole, governs the Royal Guard. But it is the king's purview if he should so choose to select his own private guard. Given the upheaval we've had over the last several years, I thought it might be a good idea to reinstate the practice."

Lord Nathers, slim, with gaunt features, stood from his seat at the other end of the table. When he spoke, he always gave the air that he was talking down to you. "With all due respect Your Majesty, you have never discussed this with us."

"And that's the beauty of this. I don't need to discuss it with you. The ruling monarch, as is written in our laws, has the sole discretion on whether or not to create a Knight. And he or she alone governs them."

More hushed murmurs and complaining echoed through the room.

Ethan rolled his eyes, but then he spoke up. "Your Majesty, I think everyone is curious as to why you would engage a King's Knight."

"Well, that's simple. I have nothing but respect for the Council. The Royal Guards are the backbone of what our country was founded on. The Royal Guard was instated to protect all those of highborn lineage. To protect our nation, they come directly from the military. Before we merged the King's Knights into the Royal Guard, they were our nation's most elite security. The Knights were meant strictly for the protection of the royal family, primarily the monarch. I think all of you can agree that of late, my family and I have come under fire. Actual, literal fire."

Not one of them could disagree with that. "Yes, Your Majesty," said Coach. "But the Knights, there is nothing to govern them."

"Except me."

"Yes, and had you had them at the time of the conspiracy, what if they'd been corrupted along the way? What if we'd lost you? Who would govern them then? Who would make sure that they upheld the laws? Before they were disbanded, there were rumors that the Knights were unscrupulous."

"Ah yes, I remember those stories. In the time of Angelus and my great-grandfather, there were some Knights who may have stepped out of line, acting on behalf of Angelus or my great-grandfather, but that's not what will happen now. I'll be picking the most elite forces to be knighted. I don't need a big force, but in addition to my own personal Knights, I'll be naming Knights to provide premium security to those in the royal family who need it."

And then it struck them.

Lews sighed. "This is about Prince Tristan."

I nodded. "The Council voted, and I respect that. The Royal Guard has come under fire. Their ranks were infiltrated. It makes sense that we should all be concerned. And as we right the ship, it makes sense that there would be those who are deemed suspicious or perhaps suspect. And as we all voted, I understand that it didn't go my way this time. But I stand by the fact that I believe my cousin needs more protection than the Council was willing to give him. And if I can do something to protect any member of my family at my own discretion, then I will. Our laws state that a commoner shall not be sent to guard a member of royalty. As you know, my father didn't always abide by this, but I understand our need for tradition at times like this. I respect it, and we voted. So, I wouldn't want to subvert that."

Coach huffed. "So, what do you think this is?"

"I'm following the letter of the law. A private security team of King's Knights of my own. There is nothing wrong or subversive about that, as our own laws dictate. If you want to perhaps attempt to revisit the law, you're welcome to. We can add that as the ending agenda item. I'll bring our cases for discussion, and we can take a vote. But it's an ancient law. Should that really be tampered with?"

More murmuring, shaking of heads, and general grumbling echoed through the room. It would be ridiculous to attempt to change the law that didn't mostly impact anything at present. It was an old law. If I wanted to assign a couple of Knights, them voting against it would scream that I didn't have their support. It would also make any of them look suspect.

"Is there anyone who would like to put that agenda item on our platform for the next vote?"

No one spoke. Eyes shifted around.

Ethan raised a brow and stared at me. I grinned back at him. "In that case, let's continue."

I had what I wanted. The Council was going to bend to my

will. And now I just needed Knights. Luckily, I knew exactly where to look.

NEELA...

Since we were eight, after my father died Willa had been basically everything to me. My whole world. She'd been my best friend, my sister, my champion.

Or at least I'd thought.

She's no champion of yours.

I had seen her last night, rubbing herself all over Jax. Neither one of them had seen me. The pit had fallen out of my stomach.

Mayzie had started to stir, so I'd woken up to rub her belly and soothe her back to sleep. I'd gotten out of the shower and heard them talking out in the living room. Neither one of them had heard me as I'd slunk out into the hallway with nothing on but my towel. I didn't know what I'd see or what I'd hear, but what I'd seen was my best friend since I was eight years old rubbing herself all over... what the hell did I even call him?

Was he my boyfriend? I didn't know what the hell was going on with us.

Your man. He is your man.

But that sounded ridiculous. We were close, and the way I felt about him... I was pretty sure I'd never felt that way before. And just like back in high school with Ian Metzer, Willa swooped in and stole him from right under my nose.

Attempted to steal him.

Jax had told her no. And in no uncertain terms. The flush of warmth was almost enough to chase to chill away.

Willa wasn't my friend. She never had been. Which meant for years, I'd been torturing myself, chasing after someone who hadn't wanted me and certainly hadn't had my best interests at heart.

That morning, Jax had taken Mayzie out to the pool in her little floaters and swim diaper. She was happy as a clam, and it was good that Jax was able to take her out. She had been a little cranky.

Willa was outside watching them from the little porch. "She got so big when I wasn't looking."

"Yeah, she did," I said as I adjusted my sunglasses. "That's what happens when you abandon your child. They grow up without you."

Her jaw unhinged. "Jesus Christ. You know why I had to leave."

"Sure. You fucked up. You made a deal with the devil and you ran. As always, you only ever think of yourself."

She turned to me and planted her hands on her hips, blond hair blowing in the breeze, looking every bit the fashion and art icon. "You know that is not true. Everyone thinks I'm selfish, but I'm not. I was thinking about Mayzie. I was thinking about you."

"Oh, yeah? Were you thinking about me last night when you climbed all over Jax? Rubbing yourself all over him like an animal in heat?"

Her mouth went slack for this imperceptible moment that seemed to last. In that second, I could see her for what she really was. I could see what everyone had been telling me my whole life. "Look I was just testing him, okay? Congratulations, he's all about you. I thought maybe he was, you know, in it for the win, the lay."

"The lay?"

"Come on, look at him. A guy like that, as good looking as he is, there is no way he can't be a player. But he turned me down, so he's certainly into you."

"You can't even hear yourself, can you? You have been selfish your whole life."

"How was I selfish? Your dad died, and I begged my parents to take you in. *Begged* them."

"Yeah, you begged them so you would have someone else to take the brunt of their abuse. You were luckily ignored. I didn't even see it. I thought you were doing me a favor. I thought you loved me."

She sighed and reached for my hair, fingering it between her thumb and forefinger. "Honey, I do love you. You have to understand, I just wanted what was best for you."

I glanced down at her hand and then back at her eyes behind the shades of her sunglasses. I wished I could see them. I wished she could see mine to see I was deadly serious. "I'm done Willa. I'm done with your bullshit. I'll help you with this because of Mayzie. Because I love that little girl. But when this is over, you and I are done. Forever."

"You wouldn't. I need you in my life."

"You have only ever needed me in your life to make you feel better about yourself. You're a poor friend. You only ever cared about yourself. It's time I did the same."

Willa got up and stomped back inside the room. But I wasn't done with her yet, so I followed and continued questioning her. "What was your end game, Willa?"

She shifted on the couch. "You have to hear me out, okay? I mean, you act like you've never been through this. Things just snowball out of control. I didn't know all of this was going to end up like this, okay?"

"I swear to God, it's like I'm dealing with a five-year-old. How is it that the baby is more responsible than you are?"

"That's low, okay? I mean, I messed up. I've made some bad choices. But as soon as we figure out who's coming after us, we can go back to normal."

"Well, what is normal exactly? I really need to understand your vision here."

"I don't know. Mayzie and I go about our normal day. No one is after us."

"Mayzie and you?" I was nowhere in Willa's picture.

"Well, I mean, you and I are in each other's lives again, which is great. Awesome. In fact, I love it. But it's not like you're her mom."

"Except that you left her to me."

She pulled back and blinked several times. "But I mean, I'm back."

"So you thought, what? You would leave her to me, I would be responsible for her and clean up your mess and then you would just go back to your life?"

"Well, okay. I didn't really think it through that far. But I *am* Mayzie's mother."

"You are, but I've been looking after her for over a month now. Where were you?"

"It was supposed to be temporary."

"When she was sick, who held her? When she was scared, who found her favorite toy and made it dance?"

Willa frowned. "I did all that stuff."

"No, *I* did."

"I mean, look, you and muscles out there are playing pretend, okay? It's not real. Sure, great boning, and you have this awesome baby to play house with. But the real truth is I'm back and I don't need you anymore. Once this is all settled, I'm going back to my life with my baby."

"So you put my whole life in upheaval, and you just expect me to go back to normal?"

"Of course. I mean, you have your boy toy out there. I'm sure you guys will still shag. I mean, you're probably shagging because of the intense connection thing with Mayzie, but at least you got some great orgasms. Then you can settle down with someone normal."

“What do you mean?”

“I mean, c’mon. No way a guy like that settles down. Guys like that are fun in the sack, but then you’ve gotta throw them back when you’ve used them up good. They are incapable of normal everyday life. Trust me, I know.”

"I'm not even sure we were ever friends."

She blinked wide hazel eyes at me. "You don't mean that.”

"Oh, I think I do. Willa, you don't think twice about people that you hurt. You have no qualms about ripping through people's lives at all. It's exhausting being your friend.I am physically exhausted."

"I'm sorry. I didn't know you felt this strongly about it."

"I do. That little girl, she's become my whole world for the last few weeks, and you walked away from her."

"For her safety."

"I know *why* you did it. I still don't think it was the right move. Not once have you ever mentioned going to the police or doing the right thing."

"See, that's your problem. Judging. Still judging. I won't make the same decisions that you do. I'm a different person."

"Yeah you're a different person. But you still look out for number one first, don’t you?"

FOURTEEN

NEELA...

I FELT like I was in a pressure cooker.

Jax had Mayzie at the pool. She was blissfully being a baby and happy to be with her favorite person in the world.

Neither one of them seemed too keen on being around Willa.

I, on the other hand, needed my life back. I called home to check on things. I made sure to use the exact protocols Ariel had showed me to use the sat phone.

Bex answered right away. "Hey, boss lady. How are things going with Mr. Man?"

She couldn't see me, but I flushed. "Mr. Man is good. Fine. Whatever. But I'm not calling to talk about him. I'm calling to talk about everything else. How is everything?"

Bex made her, 'hell yes!' squeal. "You boned? Praise be!"

God, I equal parts loved her and wanted to throttle her. "Work, okay? Where are we?"

Bex put the phone on speaker. "Adam, you're up."

I could hear the rolling of their chairs, and Adam cleared his throat. "What's up, boss lady?"

"Tell me we have something on this ledger."

"We have more than something. The program finally deciphered it all. I did my own manual checks, and it took me a little longer to double-check, but Vanhorn is either a fucking genius or a complete and total nerd. The ledger is in Klingon, Romulan and Vulcan. One language for each of the key pieces of information. And then you have to use a cipher code to decipher it. It's brilliant, actually."

"Do you want to give him a job?"

"No. I'm just saying. Okay, the real deal is, you need to know that Willa wasn't just shipping the occasional item to Vanhorn, she was his partner."

The hairs at the back of my neck stood at attention. "What do you mean?"

"Look, I've got shipment dates and names. Those names don't match with any known associates of Vanhorn's. They are her artists' names going back years."

I couldn't breathe. Oxygen was a luxury. Willa had said that she'd only gotten caught up with him a year ago. "What else did you find?"

"That's the interesting thing. It doesn't have the name of the institution or the bank, but it does have an address."

I knew where this was going. "Let me guess, the address of the gallery?"

"Bingo. He funded her from the start. The whole time before she died, she was working for him."

I swallowed the guilt. It was a need-to-know situation that Willa was still alive. I knew team Royal Elite knew, but Adam and Bex didn't need to know because that information might get them hurt. "So all along, all these years, she's been Vanhorn's money launderer?"

"Yup, that's right. And she was no dummy. When Bex and I looked further back into the gallery's history, we found that she started making deposits into a variety of accounts in Mayzie's name. Completely clean."

"Like what?"

"There is a college fund, all kinds of property, and several businesses all in Mayzie's name. Nothing to tie her back to it. The gallery receives money, and then it goes out again. So even if the authorities caught on, they can't freeze her accounts. Mayzie is untouchable. And get this, Mayzie has been paying taxes since the day she was born. As soon as her national number was created along with her birth certificate, she began earning money as a director of a board of trustees."

"A little tiny mogul."

"Exactly. That's how Willa was getting away with it. She paid her as an employee of a board of trustees of a shell company that barely exists and only on paper. Mayzie has made an incredible amount of wealth for such a young age. The baby is only a year old, and she has properties on five continents, incredible holdings, and that money is clean, clean, clean. Mayzie has been paying taxes on every dime that would be considered at all taxable. No loopholes, no fancy rigging. Willa found a way to cleanly wash her money. And I bet that she did the same for Vanhorn. Vanhorn has got three kids. How much do you want to bet that they are practically billionaires?"

I had to sit down. I eased myself onto the edge of the bed. "Jesus Christ."

"Yeah. I mean, if I was a criminal mastermind, I'd be impressed, because sure, Willa could have eventually gone to jail if she'd lived, but when she got out, she would have had access to the money, provided she had access to Mayzie."

"Okay, but she's dead, right? So no one would benefit then?"

"No, but Mayzie is well provided for."

Bex interjected. "I mean, honestly if this was a movie of the week, I'd say that Willa faked her own death, plans to come back, grab Mayzie, and get all that clean money and retire to some uninhabited island somewhere."

I swallowed hard. This was not the time to come clean about Willa still being alive. No wonder I wasn't in Willa's plans. She'd already made her own plans. She just needed me to do my part. There was one thing I didn't understand though. "Okay, so help me understand. Why did she send me the ledger?"

"I don't know," Adam said. "It doesn't make any sense. I mean, unless it wasn't Willa who sent it to you. But again, that's ridiculous because most people would have just hired you to decode the ledger."

He had a point. I consider Bipps could be dirty, but then again, why not just hire me? He'd been Willa's attorney, so why had Willa given me the journal?

"Okay, devil's advocate. If someone was looking for information on the journal, what would they be looking for? Let's not look at who would have a motive, but let's look for what the biggest secret or biggest finding in there was."

I could hear Adam rolling around in his chair. "Okay. I found probably the biggest nugget. Vanhorn has information in there about a diamond mine. It's not where you'd think you'd find a diamond mine. This one is located in Chile."

I frowned. "Chile?"

"Yep. But his name isn't on the deed."

"But, I don't get it. Why is another diamond mine not in his name important?"

"It's the name that's on the deed that matters. TRICLO investing."

I frowned. "Why do I know that name?"

"They've been in the media lately, running a lot of ads for politicians left and right in the US at the moment, most recently for some new congressman everyone says is going to be president one day."

"So dirty Vanhorn is backing politicians."

"Oh yeah, looks that way. And more importantly, that particular bit of information could be worth not just millions but billions. Every politician being backed by TRICLO would pay out the nose. And it's got TRICLO's entire client roster listed here."

I whistled low. "Holy shit."

"Yeah. So, at the end of the day, there are a lot of people who would greatly benefit by this ledger never seeing the light of day. Whoever killed Willa was deadly dangerous. You guys watch your back."

"Yeah, I hear you. Okay. You haven't told Ariel or anyone, right?"

"Nope. Bex and I are the only ones who know."

"Okay. Bex, like we talked about, make a copy of that and stash it in the yoga studio, back panel behind the tampons. Make another copy, and I want you to take it to the Central Bank. You have access to my box. I want you to put a copy in there. And then Adam, I want you to wipe our hard drives. I want no evidence whatsoever that we had any access to it. If this reaches far and wide, I don't want anyone knowing that we were able to decipher it. Do you understand me?"

There was a bit of silence. "Are you sure? Because we might need it in the future."

" Just having the information will be enough. If we ever need to decipher it again, we at least know the pattern and the code. If we could destroy the original, I would. But you guys can't get access to it. I know Ariel did something with it. For all I know, it's in the palace."

I could tell Adam wanted to dig his heels in. "I mean, she's a decent hacker. That's no doubt. But I'm not bad myself. Should I break in to her systems?"

"No. And we don't want her breaking in to your systems either. Wipe our drives."

"You never let me have any fun."

"I'm serious, you guys. The information we have is dangerous. I'm the one they want, but you guys work for me. That makes you targets too. Even worse, Richard used to work with us. He doesn't have the skillset to decipher it, but he sure knows how to access our drives."

"He can't now. I've locked everything down."

"It doesn't matter. He's a weasel if you've ever met one. I want everything clean. Nothing ties back to us, do you understand?"

"Fine. I get it," he grumbled.

"Bex, be careful."

"You got it." She was silent for a breath. "You're okay, right? You're safe and all that?"

"Yeah, of course." I needed to give her something though. They didn't know Willa was back. The Willa who had orchestrated this whole thing and been working for Vanhorn the whole time had pinned a target on my back deliberately. They didn't know that she was currently under the same roof as I was. "Yeah, I'm just worried about Mayzie."

"Is there a reason?" asked Bex. "I mean, she's okay, right? Hot bodyguard is protecting the both of you? Nothing is wrong?"

"Not sure yet. I'm just terrified if something happens to her it will be my fault."

"Hey, relax. Nothing is going to happen to Mayzie. Nothing is going to happen to you. Everything is going to be fine, okay? You have the best bodyguard money can buy."

"What about you guys? Is everything okay there?"

"Right as rain. Adam is super happy with Zia and Jameson and Tamsin. He's significantly less happy when it's Trace who is our bodyguard for the day. Granted, that makes me endlessly happy. Have you seen Trace? I mean, Jesus Christ. I haven't seen the abs yet, but I'm willing to bet money that they are excellent."

"They probably are if Jax is an indication."

"Yes, girl. You get you some ab viewing in there."

"That's not the point. The point is I didn't ask for any of this and my whole life is just turned upside down, and now I love these people that I never even intended to have in my life."

A beat of silence passed. "Uh-oh, did you say love?"

My stomach twisted. "You know what I mean. I didn't mean love."

"Are you sure about that?"

The problem with Bex was that she knew me too well. I was falling for Jax. I had already fallen. And while I couldn't fill Bex in on the Willa situation, I could give her this little piece of what was going on in my head. "I just... I don't know. I've never felt like this before. It's like when we're in the same room we orbit around each other. I'm always aware of where he is, what he's doing, exactly where he's going to move next. And he's like that with me. I can feel his eyes on me, even now. Even though I'm pissed off at him, I can feel him watching."

"Honey, that's falling in love. That's a good thing."

It was a terrible thing. Lying came too easy to him. I wanted him too much. I knew better than to want anything that badly.

The idea that I could lose him hurt worse than anything I could think of. A couple nights ago, even with the baby attached to my back, I'd gone into the fray with a weapon to save him.

"Yeah, what kind of an idiot falls in love with her bodyguard?"

"Oh, just about every heroine in history. That's how these things go. It's the hot testosterone. Hard bodies, intense stares. It's bound to happen, or at least a really epic shagging. Ask Whitney Houston in *The Bodyguard*, and in that British Netflix show. Sure enough, they banged. Add in intense emotional situations, and the banging is going to happen. The falling in love part, now that takes actual bonding, which you guys have done with Mayzie. You're like a little family. If you had a fight, work it out. You're the rational one, remember? I'm the one who's more likely to throw things. Talk it out. You're an excellent communicator. You always have been. You've just never been one to go after what you want. And finally, you have someone who wants what you want, so you need to go after him and hold on tight. If you don't, I will. That man has abs for days. I'm imagining, of course."

"He does."

Bex groaned. "Don't tease a girl, ahhh. But you, enjoy something in your life for once. You don't have to work all the time. You don't have to make everything perfect for everyone else. Make it perfect for you. Besides, you're not really mad at him. You're really mad at Willa for abandoning you."

For once, I might listen to Bex. Even if I didn't know exactly how he felt, one thing I did know was that we had to work this out. Because like it or not, we were a team. And we had to figure out what we were going to do to keep Mayzie safe. I'd figure out the feelings later.

You already know how you feel.

Okay, but I wouldn't be laying everything on the table until I knew how he felt about me too.

You already know.

Jax...

SOMETHING WAS WRONG WITH NEELA. She was quiet and withdrawn. At first, I thought it was the fight with Willa, but it was something else. Something she wouldn't tell me about.

That morning when I'd woken at five, she was already wide awake, pacing, writing down stuff in her notebook. Me being me, I'd snuck a peek. Yes, that was an invasion of privacy, but she wasn't *talking* to me.

Sure, she was letting me touch her now, but last night she'd been distracted. It had taken her longer than usual to come, and then she'd wrapped herself around me and held on tight as if she was terrified I was going somewhere.

I knew that the earlier conversation with Willa was playing in her head, or Willa made it seem like I was going to get bored with her and run. Although I'd done everything in my power to show her that that wasn't me, that I wasn't the guy who was going to run. Still, she was off. I could tell. I just wished I knew exactly what it was that was bothering her so I could assuage her worry.

Or did she see you? I'd made it clear in no uncertain terms last night that I wasn't going to touch Willa ever. But had Neela seen her friend come on to me?

If she had, why hadn't she said anything? By now she should have said something. At least I hoped she would.

It could be work. She'd been locked in on the sat phone with Bex and Adam earlier in the day, speaking in hushed tones that I couldn't really decipher or make out from the door. I knew her company had been in trouble after the breakup. I didn't know how much trouble she was in, especially now with Willa back. And the infusion of cash she'd had or been able to save by living at Willa's was probably up in the air now. That might be it, but instinct told me it was something different. It might be the ledger too.

Willa was convinced that there was something in it that would save her, and she kept pressing Neela to work harder to try and decipher it. Maybe that was it. Either way, I had to figure it out. Out on the balcony, I made my check-in call at the pre-arranged time with Ariel.

Her answer was brusque. "All good?"

"Yeah. All good. Do we have any verification on Willa MacKenzie's story?"

"No. She didn't use a single credit card, obviously. No major cash withdrawals, but she might have had some on her. She might have gotten paid in cash for more of her sculptures or something. She clearly needed money to run."

"What about Satorini?"

"What about him?"

"Willa said that the two of them stole the ledger from

Vanhorn together. And she said the relationship was volatile. He'd gotten violent, so she ghosted and came here to get her daughter, but that's not tracking. Do we have eyes on him?"

"No. He's dark as well. Although he didn't fake a death. The moment he surfaces, I'll let you know."

"Yeah, okay."

"And how is Neela?"

"A mess. She is... I don't know... tense about something. She's not talking."

Ariel was quiet for a bit. "I know I gave you a hard set of rules. I know how difficult undercover can be."

"I'm handling it." We were not having some long drawn out conversation about my love life.

Notice you said love life and not someone you're shagging.

I shoved aside the thought.

But Ariel wasn't finished yet. "Look, I know you care about that little girl, and I'm not an idiot. I know you care about Neela Wellbrook."

"You have a rule, I know."

"Rules you basically broke right away."

I bit back my chuckle. "Does this whole conversation have a point?"

"My point is I don't know if this is going how it's supposed to go. And while I think it's unwise for you to be banging the client, I know this is hard on you because you're close to it."

"I can do my job, Ariel."

"I know you can. Roone told me you were the best, and I trust him. I trust that you will bring the client home safe. I'm just saying, you don't have to be on your own. I can send someone else out there to help. I know what it's like when you get personally invested."

"Oh, the great Ariel Scott got too close to a client once?"

"More along the lines of I got too close to someone I had no business getting close to. It's why I get it. If you need help, just give a shout."

"Yeah, I hear you. But listen, something tells me Neela is tense for a reason. She has been hunched over her notebooks since we got here. She said she hasn't figured out the ledger yet, but something tells me all of this is about what's in that ledger. You said you have some of your programs trying to decipher it. Any luck?"

"No. I was just checking with Adam and Bex too. They're coming up empty."

"So what, Vanhorn is just a fucking genius? He's managed to create an uncrackable code, a code a skilled cryptanalyst cannot decipher?"

"I'm pretty sure they *can* decipher it, but it'll take time."

"We don't have time. Willa MacKenzie is alive, and she's applying pressure, which means that she's got a deadline for something, so our time is running out."

"I hear you. Maybe it's time for me to take a little look-see in Neela's hard drives. Cryptanalysts are used to secrets. Maybe Neela has been keeping some of her own."

The idea of Neela keeping secrets tasted like bile on my tongue. But it was entirely possible she and her team had already cracked the code.

Then why hasn't she told you?

I had no idea, but we needed to know what they knew.

FIFTEEN

Jax...

When I found Neela, she was pacing back and forth across the balcony, muttering to herself, and then she'd write something in a notebook that she had. Then she'd go right back to muttering and frown, and then pull something up on her computer. She was working on the ledger. I knew it. But why was she hiding it?

I could have kept watching her, but it was easier to deal with it head on. "So, are we going to talk about it?"

Her head snapped up and her eyes went wide. "Jesus, Jax, you're like a ninja."

"I wasn't even being quiet. You're just so engrossed in thought."

"Sorry. Is Mayzie okay?"

I nodded. "She's taking a nap."

"Okay, good." She frowned then. "Has, um, you know, Willa spent any time with her? I've been so busy with work the last couple of days, I haven't been paying attention. I want Mayzie to know that her mom loves her."

I studied her for a moment. "I know what you'd like. I'm just not sure whether or not it's true."

She frowned as she rubbed the back of her neck. "Jax, just give it a rest, okay? Regardless of how *you* feel about Willa, she's Mayzie's mom."

There was a hint of bite to the way she said 'you' and she refused to meet my gaze. She knew. Watching her warily, I asked, "So, you saw?"

She frowned at me. "Saw what?"

"Willa the other day. Rubbing all over me like a cat in heat."

Her face flushed a slight hint of pink under her tanned skin. "You don't have to explain anything to me. You're not tied down to me in any way."

Was she out of her mind? That's what the problem was. "Have you fucking lost the plot?"

Her brows snapped down. "Excuse me?"

Oh, she'd heard me. To make sure, I enunciated for her. "The plot, have you lost it? You and I. I told you from the very beginning... You, me, that we were happening."

"Well, what am I supposed to think? After all, you would just be the next in a very long line of men who prefer Willa MacKenzie to me."

I stepped forward into her space until I was crowding her. But I needed her to hear me, to feel me. "Willa came on strong. I imagine that's what she does. I turned her down, and she got defensive."

She continued holding her shoulders stiff. "You don't need to explain anything to me."

"Well, obviously, I do." I clenched my jaw. "I know trust between us is fragile. I broke it before we even began. And I can't go back and fix that. I can't do anything to mend it, except give you my word that every day that we are together, I am all-in with you. I have zero interest in Willa, and she knew it. She still gave it a go, but she knew. I can't get *you* out of my bloody head. *You* are the one I dream about. *You* are the one who's scent I can't get off my tongue. *You.* No one else. So, I don't want Willa MacKenzie. She's obvious. She tries too hard. And she's desperate. You are none of those things. And you are so much more."

Her lips parted, and her gaze skittered downward. "You don't have to say all of this. It doesn't matter."

"Yes, it does. Because I think maybe no one has ever said it to you before. You are not my bloody second choice. From the moment I saw you, you were the *first* choice. Honestly, the *only* choice. I didn't touch her. And I know that you don't necessarily need to hear that, but I need to tell you. I would never."

She blinked her eyes rapidly and gave me a small nod. "I just —I saw you two, and it was like my whole life all over again."

"I really wish you'd said something last night. For you and I, trust isn't going to come easy. But we need to work on it."

"I know. It's just that we're new, and this would not be the first time someone has, you know, seen Willa and decided they got the short end of the stick with me."

"I don't know who the hell these people were, but I'll kill them. Every last one."

"Not necessary."

"We have to trust each other. I know it's easy to say that, but we do. With everything going on right now, it's you and me and Mayzie. Do you understand?"

She nodded. "Yeah. Sorry, I was just—It wasn't easy seeing you like that."

"If I'd seen some guy on you, I might have killed him. Since we're being honest."

"Well, okay, that's good to know."

"It took everything in my power not to kill your stupid ex."

"I might have liked to watch that."

"Bloodthirsty." I dropped my forehead to hers and met her gaze, letting her scent whirl around us and lock me into place. "Now, tell me what the hell is going on because I know something is up. Something more than Willa. Something important. Is it the ledger?"

I saw it in her eyes. The moment when she decided to tell me some of it, if not all. She was still holding something back. But I'd take the small victory today.

"I don't want to say anything yet, but we have almost decoded it, the ledger. Dates, times, when it was done. The last thing I want is for Willa to know. I don't trust her. And so far, what I'm seeing in that ledger doesn't make her the victim. It makes her the perpetrator in all of this."

I clenched my jaw. "You need to tell me things like that."

"I can't. I don't have the full picture yet. The ledger is not done."

I sighed. "If you have any proof at all that she's bad news, we'll drop her like a bad habit."

Neela chewed her lip. "Or we keep her around so at least we have our eyes on her. Until I have the whole ledger decoded, we can't do anything. And until it's all decoded, she still needs me. The problem is that the piece that Willa has, the additional cipher she's been talking about, it only works with the physical book at hand, so I won't get all the final names in that ledger until I actually have the book."

I cursed under my breath. "Right now, that book is under lock and key."

"I know. I have the copies that we made, and Willa's cipher might do the trick. I don't know. But something tells me we're going to need the originals. There is some kind of stamp embossed on some of the pages. It's like a hidden text, I guess. I need Willa's cipher to be able to crack it. And I need the original fucking ledger."

I cursed under my breath. "Ariel has got it for safekeeping."

"I know. And something tells me it's probably a bad idea if I actually decode it, because then I won't be necessary anymore. Then I'll just be an obstacle."

I clenched my jaw. "I would kill her before I let anything happen to you."

She frowned and shook her head. "No. No one is going to die for me. But we need to keep a close eye on Willa because she is in this up to her eyeballs."

Her hands shook, and I tugged her close, encapsulating them in my far bigger ones. "Look, you and I will figure this out. We're not going to let anything happen to Mayzie."

"I wish I'd never gotten that damned ledger. All I want to do is give it back. I want my life back. I want Mayzie's life back."

All I could do was hold her tight. "I know. I swear to you, we'll figure this out." I just prayed I wasn't lying to her.

Jax...

THE DAY out was both necessary and good for us. Given the conversation Neela and I had about Willa, I couldn't leave

Neela at home. I certainly wouldn't leave Mayzie with Willa without any coverage. So that meant Neela and Mayzie had to come with me, which left Willa all on her own.

I'd bugged the place, but she was still there alone. Free to set us up or do God knew what.

"You think this is a bad idea?" Neela asked as I pushed Mayzie in the spare stroller we'd borrowed from the hotel. Our shopping bags were laden with food as we walked back.

"You know, I'm not sure yet. It could be fine. Maybe Willa had been bad news, got mixed up with the wrong people, and had a change of heart. There is a slim chance she could be telling the truth."

"Okay, then is there a reason you won't leave me alone with her?"

"I couldn't guarantee you wouldn't kill her."

Her lips quirked. "You know what, that's entirely accurate. She was all over you. I didn't like it."

"My, my, you are possessive."

"What, and you aren't?"

I shrugged. "I never said that. I feel like I made it perfectly clear. I'd kill anyone who had his hands on you."

"Kill is such a strong word."

I shrugged. "Maybe it's strong, but it's accurate."

As we passed the streets along Queen's Way, something caught my eye in the reflection of a window. A blue sedan. Had I seen it before? Was I being paranoid? Better safe than sorry. I maneuvered us around until we made a left further into the cluster of shops and cafes.

For a moment, Neela didn't even seem to notice. She just walked along as if she had not a care in the world, enjoying the sunshine, relaxing. It was only after we made another turn heading back toward the beach that she frowned. "Are we walking in a circle?" I noticed a Volkswagen Beetle make the same two turns that we did. They had us in a two-car follow pattern. It didn't matter. I was going to end that now.

"Are you partial to the stroller?"

Neela frowned at me. "What?"

"The stroller, do we really need it?"

"No. I guess not. I mean, we have the carriers."

I stopped the stroller and unlatched the baby. Mayzie laughed because she thought we were playing a game. She was less than thrilled though when I put her in the carrier we had brought and strapped her in, tight. She preferred to have a better range of motion. But it couldn't be helped. Neela didn't even ask any questions. Instead, she just grabbed the diaper bag and the shopping bags and looked to me. "Lead the way."

If I wasn't already half in love with the woman, that would have sealed the deal. She brooked no arguments, asked no questions, just did whatever she needed to do to get the job done. I took them to the older part of the city, where the restaurants were more closely packed together. Once we hit an alleyway behind one of the buildings, I cupped my hand around Mayzie's head, and we sprinted up above the embankment, over and up into the residential area. I scrambled over the wall first, Mayzie in tow, careful to project her as I climbed and when I landed. Neela came next. When I took her hand, she squeezed gently to let me know she trusted me, and then we were running again through the cobbled streets, through the pedestrians, the tourists, and the street vendors.

I ran a route parallel to the street we would have taken, except it was more hidden. I'd been so fucking daft. It was my bright idea to not take the car because I wanted us to walk and get some exercise. Who did that? I bloody knew better. Finally, we hit the back of the hotel. I made a foothold for Neela and I hoisted her up over the back fence. It was far too high for me to climb with Mayzie, so I unstrapped her and handed her back over to Neela. Then I climbed up myself.

When I landed in the sand, I breathed a sigh of relief. No matter what, at least no one had seen us come back here. Either way, we needed to leave. But at least we were safe for the moment, and we'd have some breathing room.

We marched back into the suite. Willa glanced up from her magazine. "Back so soon?"

I didn't bother with niceties. I'd bloody had it. "Pack your things. We need to leave. We've been compromised."

SIXTEEN

JAX...

Willa MacKenzie had to go.

I was more than convinced she'd signaled someone. I just didn't know how yet. She had no phone, and I'd checked her for bugs and trackers. I hadn't found anything.

But it didn't matter, I knew what had happened. Now I had to find a way to get her the hell away from Neela and Mayzie. I just had to figure out how to keep Neela from having something to say about it.

Good luck with that.

Yeah, Neela was definitely going to have something to say. She didn't trust Willa either, but she wanted Mayzie to get to know her mum. Even though she knew Willa well, she would always err on the side of what was good for the baby.

Didn't matter. I had to find a way to separate us from the problem. Next chance I had, I'd need to call home base and have one of the team come and collect Willa. I was done dicking around.

Our next stop was a little small for three adults and a baby. Willa glanced around. "Where am I supposed to sleep?"

I glowered at her. "There is the couch."

"I don't understand why we just can't stay in a hotel."

I leveled a gaze on her. “We tried that already. And then your friends showed up. We need to keep a low profile."

Her eyes went wide. “Are you suggesting I had something to do with them finding us? How? You had my phone. You took the clothes I arrived in. I couldn’t possibly have signaled anyone.”

“There are still ways.”

Neela rocked the baby in her arms as she paced the entrance of the tiny kitchenette. “Would you both stop? Please. It’s not helping.”

Willa sighed. "Whoever is coming, is coming for me. I recognize I fucked up. I never should have sent you the ledger, Neela. But if I just volunteer to hand over the ledger, at least Vanhorn’s men will go away. Michael will be another matter, but I’ll deal with him when I deal with him. Or I’ll go to the authorities. I mean, I’ve seen a lot. Certainly enough to put him away."

I couldn’t believe what I was hearing. “You’re going to hand it back? Are you mad? We still don't know everything it says. We’re not going to do that until Neela has more time to decipher it. We need proper leverage, a way out of this mess you put her in. We hand it back to Vanhorn now, and we lose all leverage. Nothing’s to stop his men from killing us all. Best bet is to go back with the strength of the team behind us.”

“I might as well be a sitting duck if I go back with nothing to show for it. I’m either making a play with the ledger or I need to stay dead.”

I really did not like this woman.

Hate was a strong word, but I didn't care for her. She was a liar. Every word out of her mouth had been a lie since we'd embarked on this little adventure. Not to mention, baby Mayzie was not too keen on her mum. Every time Willa picked her up, there were tears. And then she would dive for my arms saying, "Da."

Of course, there was a part of me that wanted to believe she was trying to say Daddy.

Yeah, that's the dumb part, mate.

It was the part of me that wanted to believe. It was stupid. Emotions like that could get everyone hurt. Emotions would shift my focus, and I couldn't afford that right now.

Another huge risk. I still couldn't help it though. From the moment I'd first held that kid, I'd felt like she was mine, which was stupid, I was well aware.

Because she wasn't.

Willa continued her hard press for the idea. "Look, we might as well hand it over. I haven't seen Neela with it at all."

"What the hell do you think she's been doing half the time?"

Willa slid a glance over to Neela who was hunched over her phone. "Where is it?"

Neela glanced up. "We didn't think it was safe to carry, so I stashed it. But took photos so I've been able to work on it."

Willa pushed to standing as she stared at me. "You mean you don't have it *with* you?"

I shook my head. "Of course not."

"Neela?" Willa asked.

"It's safe."

Willa refused to back down. "No. I'm sorry, but it's my life, I'm not leaving it in the hands of anyone else. I'll just go get it."

I laughed. "Well, I'm not letting you go anywhere unsupervised. What's to stop you from taking off with that ledger? Any answers we need will go with you."

"Neela can come with me. She needs to work on it anyway."

The fuck? "My directive is clear. Keep Mayzie and Neela safe."

Willa squared her shoulders. "Actually no. Your directive is to keep *Mayzie* safe. Not Neela."

My brows snapped down. "What?"

"Look, there's only *one* of you. I didn't want the baby in danger. It's faster and safer if you stay here with Mayzie."

"Let me be clear with you, love. Where Neela goes, I go. You aren't to be trusted."

"Oh for the love of Christ. If you—"

Neela interrupted. "Jesus Christ. Would the two of you stop?"

"Neela—" I started, but she gave me a sharp shake of her head.

"Bedroom now." She handed a sleeping Mayzie over to Willa. "Put her down."

Willa's brows drew up. "We're not done. We can't put this off any—"

"We are done. I *am* done. We just fled armed assailants... *again*. And you two are busy yelling at each other. I never asked for any of this. I'm tired. Jax, bedroom. Now."

Why was it so hot having her give me orders? Maybe because I had full intention on challenging those orders once we were in the bed.

But that was not what she had in mind when she slammed the door behind us. "You have to stop."

I stared at her. "What? I thought we were on the same page here?"

"We are, but I can't take the constant push and pull.

"I hear you. We'll make sure that—"

She shook her head vehemently. "I want it done. Let me just give her the ledger. The sooner she has it, the sooner she'll be out of our hair. We both know she doesn't really want Mayzie."

"So you want to just give it up? No telling what that information is. What it could mean. Who it could hurt. No. It's better if I call Ariel, and we take her somewhere to be questioned. And I can keep you safe."

"Yeah but for how long? They'll keep coming. Vanhorn. Satorini. Whoever else she pissed off. I didn't want this. My father's life is now my life. He was always looking over his shoulder. I was adamant that I wanted nothing to do with that. I need simplicity in my life. I'll give the ledger to Willa, then everything goes back to the way it was before."

I scrubbed a hand down my face. "No. This is insane. You finish the translation and you are a sitting duck."

"If I don't finish and I don't hand it off, I'm a sitting duck anyway. Jax, I just want Mayzie to be safe." Her voice quavered. "Sh—she's everything. And I don't know if I'll survive knowing I could have done something to save her and I didn't."

I tugged her close. "We'll call in reinforcements in the morning. We might need to take the fight to home base since obviously they keep finding us. You're bone weary. We can't think like this with only half the picture. Let's talk to the team in the morning. We'll get the full lay of the land. Besides. You don't have the journal. Ariel has got it for safe keeping. Once we talk to everyone we'll decide okay?"

I thought she might argue, but then her shoulders sagged. "I'm so scared Jax."

"I know love. I know."

"I'm afraid I'm going to wake up in the morning and discover that I have failed Mayzie May."

"You will never have failed her. You love her too much, okay?"

"It's going to hurt so bad when she takes her away."

I dropped my forehead to hers. "Good thing, I have no intention of letting that happen."

Neela...

JAX WAS TRYING to kill me... with sex. Kill me with sex and make sure I couldn't move. Because if I couldn't move, then it meant I wasn't going anywhere.

And he knew I was going.

I'd been deprived of sleep by the most delicious sensations. That tugging and pulling of my breasts, and that low pull in my belly. It was some kind of delicious friction.

I woke up to find Jax with his mouth around my nipple and his fingers sliding between my lips, gently circling my clit.

"Morning love," he said, intermittently switching his mouth between my two breasts.

After we'd made love half the night, I'd slept fitfully. I knew what had to be done about Willa. I knew my part in it. I just knew I'd have to do the one thing Jax didn't want me to do.

Not that I wanted to do it either.

But the more I thought about it, I knew the fastest way to

end this was to give Willa what she wanted. Then she'd be out of our lives. I'd make her see a life on the run was no life for a baby. Besides, I wasn't above bargaining with Willa to keep Mayzie safe. I'd do anything.

I was still too much in my head, and Jax wasn't having a moment of that. He nipped me gently on the nipple, making me cry out. "Jax."

"Focus love. I'm the one giving you orgasms. We have plenty of time to worry later."

Before I knew it, I was moaning, and I couldn't give two fucks if Willa heard us.

Jax wasted no time. He slid under the covers, palming my ass in both hands and spreading me wide. "No time for preamble, darling. Mayzie is going to be awake soon. I want to make sure we get our fill."

And then he planted his lips on me. He wasn't gentle. He wasn't slow. He didn't take his time. Oh no, it was fast, flat licks with his tongue, the occasional grazing with his teeth, the sliding in of his fingers, fucking me quickly. No gentle slide, no calm wake-up. He wanted orgasms and he wanted them immediately. And I was going to give them to him, whether I wanted to or not.

Spoiler alert. I totally wanted to.

"Jax—"

"Yeah, love?"

How could he be so calm? I felt like fire was racing through my veins, ready to combust, ready to blow me up from the inside.

Just when I was close enough that I could taste it, I could feel it, he stopped.

"Jax—"

"Shh. I'm right here." His lips brushed mine, and I could taste myself on them. Just the knowledge of what he'd been doing was enough to have me raising my hips, trying to meet the slide of his erection. I needed that delicious friction.

"Shit. Love. Do we have enough condoms left?"

I frowned. "I'm on the pill."

His eyes went wide. "What?"

"The pill, I never went off."

Jax muffled a curse against my lips. He grabbed his erection at the base and then smoothed it over my clit.

I threw my head back. "Oh my God."

"That's how you make me feel. Every damn day. Just on the edge of bursting because I need to be with you."

"What are you doing, Jax?"

"That's easy. I'm loving you."

And then he pressed his tip inside and watched as he slid into me. His eyes were on us joining. My eyes were on him. The exaltation on his face was incredible to watch.

"You own every part of me."

And then he was moving. Quickly. Just like all those fascinating porn movies I'd ever seen, where the guy had the girl basically pinned to the bed with his hips and he was working her over.

But unlike the girls in those videos, I was enjoying the ride. I didn't have much range of motion in my hands, but I could arch my back, trying to get him to give me what I wanted.

It was delicious. I loved it. He sank so deep, and he was so big, stretching me. It was all I wanted. It was all I maybe was ever going to need. Him, inside me, knowing every inch of me.

With a rough snarl, he flipped us over, squeezing my ass tightly as he held me on top of him.

I sucked in a sharp breath when the tip of one of his fingers grazed over my anus.

He gave me a devilish grin. "Did you like that?"

"I—uh—"

He did it again, more firmly this time, and his touch coincided with a slide of his thickness inside me. "Oh my God. Oh my God. I—"

"Is that a yes?"

"Yes, it's a yes. Oh, Jesus."

And then he was sliding a finger inside my ass as he was still inside me. He slid his free hand into my hair and gripped. A tiny sting of pain only heightened what I was feeling. He was owning me, possessing me.

Jax pulled my hair back, forcing me to arch my back, forcing my breasts to be an offer for him, and then he leaned up and took one into his mouth as he stimulated the most sensitive parts of my body.

Before I knew it, I was flying. With his finger in my ass, his cock deep inside me, the bare slide of nothing between us, I broke apart. Teeth biting my lip, bliss coursing through me, I fell. Completely and totally in love.

He wasn't done with me though.

He only increased his pace, sucked harder, pulled more. Finally, he released my breast, his teeth diving into that soft spot on my shoulder between my ear and the hollow of my neck, and he bit me, roaring into it as he came. His body jerked beneath mine. His arms tightened around me. His finger that had been doing all those dirty things to me, gently tapped that bundle of nerves, making me shake and shudder.

"Jesus Christ, Neela, you're fucking going to kill me."

"I'm pretty sure I'm already dead. So, I beat you."

"Woman."

I wanted to stay in his arms. I wanted to just do nothing more than this and let him make love to me every day.

But I knew I had to go. Willa had the missing piece of the ledger. And with people on our trail, she was the key to cracking everything. She was also the key to that little girl's safety. I had to get her as far away from Mayzie as possible. If Jax had to stick with Mayzie, I would take Willa. And I knew just how to do it.

Lazily stroking his hand up my back, Jax kissed my mouth first, then my cheeks, and I said, "I'm going to get some water. You want a sports drink?"

He started to sit up abruptly. "I'll do it."

I pushed him back down. "Nope. You take care of me all the time. I can do it."

He smile was immediate. "Thank you."

"Anytime. I want you to know I still expect to be waited on hand and foot when we get back."

His low, rumbling chuckle made me contemplate another round. But no. If I didn't pull the trigger now, I never would.

In the kitchen, I grabbed myself a glass of water and him a drink from the fridge. I hoped to God the drinks were sweet enough to mask the bitterness. I then marched into the bathroom of the cramped safehouse and grabbed the sleeping pills in the medicine cabinet. I didn't know the dosage. I just needed to put him out long enough to leave with Willa. He was determined to do everything his way.

My way might be bat-shit crazy, but at least my way would get rid of Willa, not make her an even bigger problem.

When I returned to the bedroom, I pretended to open the bottle and handed it over. He didn't even blink and guzzled it down.

He would be pissed in the morning. But he'd eventually understand. He would have to.

"Come back to bed, love. Let me hold you. It's still a few minutes until dawn and Mayzie will be up."

"Okay. You twisted my arm." I snuggled in, reveling in the feel of him.

"I love you. You know that," he mumbled as he kissed my shoulder.

"I love you too, Jax." I just hoped he forgave me.

An hour later as his snores filled the silence, I slunk out from under his arm and dressed in a hurry. When I snuck out to the living room, I found Willa on her back, half falling off the couch. I shook her awake.

"What the fuck, Neela?"

"If you want the ledger, now is the time to get it. Move your ass. One condition, though; You leave Mayzie with me until you sort out your shit. She needs stability, and you know that."

"You're shitting me. You expect me to give up my daughter?"

I lifted my chin. "I expect you to clean up your mess and not drag her into it. Your choice. That's the only way we're doing this."

Willa glowered at me but then gave me a sharp nod. "Fine."

"Get ready to go, we don't have much time."

She blinked several times as if she didn't believe me, but then she got her ass in gear.

While Willa dressed, I went over to the baby cot in the corner and kissed Mayzie's forehead. "I love you, Mayzie May. You be good for Jax. I'll see you soon."

I just prayed I wasn't making a huge mistake. Under cover of darkness, I left behind my family, hoping to keep them safe.

SEVENTEEN

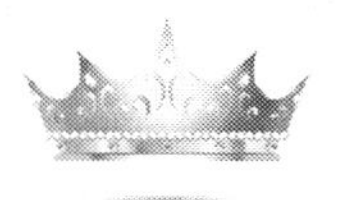

JAX...

At first I thought it was Mayzie that woke me up. But no. That scratching sound wasn't the baby. I dragged open my eyes, reached for the weapon underneath my pillow, and stayed very quiet.

Fuck, I was lethargic. My eyes weren't working right. They didn't want to stay open. Not to mention I was groggy, and my mouth felt like it was stuffed with cotton.

The fuck?

You've been drugged.

Shit. Mayzie. I had to get to Mayzie. Had Willa drugged me?

I patted the other side of the bed for Neela, but the sheets were cool. She'd been out of bed a long time.

My brows furrowed as I tried to make the synapses fire correctly.

Slowly, it dawned. It wasn't Willa who'd drugged me. It had been *Neela*.

I glowered at the sports drink on the night stand. She'd

drugged me. She'd fucking drugged me and nuzzled in next to me.

Worse, I knew exactly why she'd done it, and I had no idea how much time I had to stop her. I picked my phone up and sent the SOS signal to Ariel with a quick message to watch for Neela.

That woman was stupidly stubborn, and when I got my hands on her, I was going to give her the spanking of a lifetime.

There was another scraping sound. I had trouble. I went to Mayzie's bed and lifted her out of the makeshift crib, grabbed a carrier, and strapped her in. She was almost too big for it, but I had to use what we had. Then, I put her in the closet, praying that she stayed asleep.

"You stay in here, love. Uncle Jax will be right back, okay? Don't you go waking up on me."

Once she was in the closet, I grabbed my weapons. Ankle holster, back holster, and knives.

I edged closer and closer to the door. The bedroom was small. I didn't have a lot of places to hide, and the darkness was not my friend. I didn't have the night vision goggles and maybe whoever was trying to get in here did.

My watch buzzed. It told me someone had breached one of the entrances, but unfortunately, it didn't tell me which one. We had a bathroom window and the windows in the bedroom, and I had set up makeshift alarms there and on the front door. I thought the bedroom was safe. The front door was closed, so I aimed the gun toward the bathroom. I crashed forward quickly, eyes on the swivel, watching carefully. Someone was here.

"Oh, I do want to say thank you for looking after my daughter."

I scowled and then I slowly turned.

"I'm Michael Satorini. You've given us a merry chase. But now my men and I are going to take my daughter."

"How the fuck did you get in here?"

"Oh, you think I wasn't already in here? I've been hiding in that closet in that bathroom down the hallway. I've been hiding in plain sight ever since the love of your life left. Tell me, was that Willa or Neela? I know from experience just how good Willa is, how you're seeing stars, worshipping at the altar of sheer greatness. You slept with the goods, huh?"

"What the fuck do you want?"

"Just what's mine."

I don't know why it just dawned on me, the way Willa had said the name, the way she had explained they had history. He was Mayzie's father.

"You can't have her."

"You can't stop me."

"The hell I can't." I charged for him. I managed to get in a jab and a hook.

He blocked the next hook. Then he kicked me in the chest.

I coughed, but it didn't even slow me down.

I went after him again, still raw and hurting. All I could think of was that I'd promised to keep Mayzie safe. I'd promised to keep Neela safe. But I'd miscalculated somewhere. This whole time, from the moment Willa showed up, I knew it wasn't a coincidence or an accident. She had always meant to meet up with us. And Satorini showing up was a consequence of that.

"You can't have the baby. You'll have to kill me first."

And then there was a prick right in my neck. I tried to stay on my feet. Mayzie. Poor Mayzie. I had to get to her. But when I took a step forward, my knees didn't go the way they were supposed to. They were on lock, and I couldn't force the muscles around them to engage.

Then I was falling. Falling down the rabbit hole, unable to reach the white rabbit.

"Well, I'll tell you what, Mr. Reynolds. I'll leave you here to wonder where you fucked up in your life, and I'll take my daughter. Thank you very much."

"Fuck you."

"Wish I could say I was sorry, Mr. Reynolds, but you know how it is. Children belong with their parents." Then he aimed his gun and shot me twice in the chest.

The darkness took me quickly. It didn't matter how hard I fought, I'd failed both my girls.

NEELA...

The boat ride back to the main island was a quiet one. Instead of taking the ferry, Willa had managed to get us a private charter on the kind of vessel no one would go looking for if it sank.

Eventually, Willa leaned over. "Where is your sense of adventure, Neela? This could be fun."

"Only you would think that this was fun." I was worried about Jax. I was worried about Mayzie. Would either of them forgive me for leaving?

Probably not. But if I could keep Willa from bringing more pain to Mayzie's door, I had to do it.

She stayed silent after that. I couldn't help but wonder if Jax was right about her. Willa and I had been friends since we were children. She was always the wild, untamed one. But was she still my friend?

Whatkind of friend puts you in danger? What kind of mother puts her own child in danger to save her own skin?

I had to ask those questions. Because no matter what I did, I couldn't see things the way that Jax saw them. I could only remember the Willa who would stand up for me, who'd battle her mother to let me have some freedom. The Willa who told boys she wasn't going to date until someone asked me out. That was the Willa I saw when I looked at her.

But if I was being honest with myself, it had been a long time since I had seen that Willa. This Willa, I did not know.

Once we were on the main island, we flagged a taxi, and I directed it to where I'd had Bex stash the decoded ledger pages. I had the phone copies, of course, but I didn't think Willa would be satisfied enough by those to finally put an end to our nightmare.

It didn't matter. I had to have faith no one would get hurt. That was the terrible choice that I had to make. But one step at a time. Willa might know what to do with the information we'd decoded when she saw what was in it.

When we jumped out of the taxi, Willa glanced around. "Where the hell are we?"

"You said you wanted to go to the ledger, so that's where we're going."

"At some yoga studio? Jesus, anyone could have access."

"Really?"

"Yes. This isn't very secure. What if someone saw you go in here?"

"Well, for starters, I had Bex store them here, if you don't mind."

"You let that ridiculous assistant of yours hide something that important?"

"She's not just my assistant. And Bex is a whole lot more trustworthy than..." I stopped myself. I wasn't there to judge Willa. I was going to get her what she needed, and then we could go back to our lives. Me, Mayzie, and Jax.

Yes, but how does Willa fit into that happy family picture?

With the key I'd found in Willa's house, I opened the back-door to the yoga studio she owned.

"This is very reckless." Said Willa. "You have no idea what the ledgers are worth."

"I've got a good idea."

Hopefully, I was doing the right thing. Inside the studio, I turned off the alarm, and shut the door behind us. Then I led her down to where I told Bex to hide the ledgers. Outside the bathroom, Willa tapped her foot impatiently. "We are running out of time. Why on earth did you stash the ledger here?"

I'd paid for a membership when Willa first bought the studio, and I had just kept it up. Even though the studio was closed, they still had open rooms for use if you had a membership code.

I tapped in my code from memory and mumbled, "Well, it seemed like the perfect hiding place."

"You hid them in here? But I haven't been here in years. Why do you still come here?"

Rolling my eyes, I tugged open the side door and answered her. "I know you're surprised I would do anything without your express permission. But, yes, I still come here. Too lazy to cancel I guess. And I'm grandfathered in at old pricing."

Willa rolled her eyes. "Don't be so melodramatic. I didn't mean that you shouldn't still come here. I'm just surprised."

I opened the door and led the way to the bathroom. "Like you used to always say, no grown man I know would voluntarily go near a tampon dispenser. I had Bex hide the documents in a bag and seal them. Just in case they were necessary."

Willa cracked a laugh. "What? Where I used to stash my party favors?"

“Drugs. The word you're looking for is drugs.”

“God if you were so upset with what I was doing, why did you ever hang out with me?”

I shook my head. “You won’t ever get it will you? You were family to me. I always figured I could keep you out of trouble. Guess I failed.”

She was silent at that. After all, what could she say? Finally, she said, "But the ledger. It’s safe, isn’t it?"

I hoped to God it was. I was counting on the translations getting Willa on her way. “Yes,” I lied. “But remember, if I give this to you, you need to do whatever you're gonna do with it and get this danger away from Mayzie. Sort it out, Willa. Mayzie doesn’t deserve this.”

She rocked on her feet. “Yeah, fine. Whatever.”

I opened the dispenser and reached behind the back panel and pulled out the scanned copies of the ledger.

Willa frowned at me. "That isn’t the ledger."

"Oh, I know."

"Are you fucking kidding me? I need the real goddamned ledger. Not copies."

"This is the ledger. The photocopied first half of it."

"Are you fucking serious right now? You are playing with my life here."

"I promise you, I'm not. Everything you need is in these documents."

"I need the *actual* fucking ledger. And from the looks of it, this is only half. I need the whole thing, Neela. They will fucking kill me if I don't have it. This doesn't have the fucking account numbers. Everything hinges on that and the other cipher. It was going to give us TRICLO!"

A ball of ice formed in my gut as the truth seeped in. "What do you need the account numbers for? This is enough to take to the authorities. Or at the very least buy you some time."

Willa paced and ran her hands through her hair, tugging at the darker roots. "Fuck, Neela. Why do you always have to fucking do this? Why?"

She stared at me, and then she reached behind her back. Shit. I knew what was coming. "When did you figure it out?"

"I wasn't sure, honestly. But Jax knew. And you solidified my concerns when you weren't over the moon to have Mayzie back. When you weren't more concerned with her safety than yours. When you described how you'd gotten away. More importantly, I know that Jax was on the king's detail and practically an expert at losing a tail. Not to mention he grew up in these islands, so he knows every nook and cranny. No way could you have followed us to King's Island."

She sighed. "You've known all along."

"I hoped I was wrong. But the guy who attempted to grab me off the street... I could have sworn I saw him following us yesterday. He had a tattoo on his left wrist of a bird or something? Maybe a swallow? He's Mayzie's father, isn't he?"

Willa cursed under her breath and pulled the gun out from behind her back. "How did you know?"

"Again. You gave yourself away. You have the same tattoo on your right shoulder now. Not to mention, the decals on Mayzie's walls are of swallows. I put two and two together. I knew as soon as I saw him that I had to get you away from her."

"Fuck. Why are you always so damn smug? All you had to do was get the ledger, figure it out, and hand it over. But no, you always thought you were better than me. A better person."

"Newsflash, I'd never put Mayzie in danger because of money."

"I'm doing this for her. I owe a lot of money. And those properties are in her name. I can't sell them, so what was I supposed to do?"

"You shouldered too much risk. That's on you. You wanted to steal the money that's in those accounts. You needed my brain to do it."

"Look, it's not personal."

"Oh, it's extremely personal. This is about a good old-fashioned heist, and the friend you used so you could get access. Well, I'm not helping you."

"Oh, you're not helping me? Even for Mayzie? You can have the baby. I just need the money so I can disappear."

"Well, I would very much love for you to disappear. But I can't decode that for you without the actual other half of the ledger."

She waved the gun at me. "I swear to God, I will kill you."

"Yeah, but then I can't decode it for you at all, can I?"

"You will, because if you don't, I'll go back to that pretty little boy toy you have, and I'll kill him. I'll kill Mayzie too."

I flinched. "She's your daughter."

"I never wanted a kid. She's a baby. I'll just drop her off to the nearest fire station. I don't care. I want the ledger. And you're going to give it to me."

"You would not hurt Mayzie."

"Can you be sure of that? You better take me to it, or you're dead. I assume it was Bex who hid it for you? Call her."

"I'm not calling her."

"Call her, or I'll kill you. It's really simple."

"Do you think I'm afraid to die?"

"No, but I think you're afraid of what I'll do to Jax and Mayzie, so call."

She handed me her phone. I knew I'd played the wrong hand and Jax had been right all along. Willa had never been my friend. She'd always been using me. And now I'd put my whole family in danger.

EIGHTEEN

JAX...

THE GRAY in my vision started to fade away as I came to.

Motherfucker that hurt.

Thank God for Ariel's rule #1. *If you're on the job, unless you're sleeping, wear a fucking vest.*

And thank God, the vest had taken the majority of that hit. My brain started to clear. My fingertips were numb and tingly. But everything moved the way it was supposed to. My chest hurt like a son of a bitch, but that was bound to happen. I tried a tentative breath. It hurt, but it was somewhat manageable. And then I lifted my hand.

No blood. The vest took both hits. But no doubt I was going to sport one hell of a bruise.

Mayzie.

Shit. I rolled to my side and pushed myself up. I managed to crawl to the closet to get the baby. But she wasn't there.

That motherfucker had taken her.

I ran for the sat phone, pulling it out from the compartment under the bedside table. I dialed quickly even as I ran to open my laptop.

In times like this, it was important to have a backup plan.

Ariel answered right away. "What's your status? I sent a car to the ferry landing after I got your SOS, But Zia and Tamsin haven't seen them yet."

"I was hoping you were going to tell me some good news.She should have been there by now."

"No dice."

"Shit."

"What's wrong on your end?"

"What's wrong is someone shot me and took Mayzie. I'm going after her."

Ariel used some inventive swearing I hadn't heard since my military days. "How? I need someone to tell me what the fuck is going on."

"I think I was right. Mommy dearest is bad news. The guy who helped her steal the ledger and fake her death and who tried to kidnap Neela is the one who took Mayzie. Michael Satorini. He's also Mayzie's dad, so it's one fucked-up family reunion. Then when Willa was safely out of the picture, we got visitors again. I'm not really one for coincidence."

"You think this is about Neela after all?"

"It has to be."

"She needed Neela to decode that ledger because she couldn't do it herself." I could hear Ariel typing on the other end.

I rubbed the back of my neck as I checked to make sure the tracker was on. Next, I strapped up with weapons. "Yeah, but there is no guarantee that Neela would be able to decode it. If she hadn't found the cipher, it would never have happened."

"She would have always found the cipher. My theory is that

Vanhorn was one of those callers about a missing piece of inventory. It prompted her to look in the gallery. And maybe that was Willa's plan."

Fuck, my head. I needed to clear it. "Okay, so Willa and Satorini pull off the heist. Steal the ledger from Vanhorn for a client. Except they decide to keep it for themselves and remove the middle man. They have the ledger, they have the cipher, but they can't read it. The heat gets too close, so they decide to go dark. Pretty hard to run with a kid, so of course Willa fakes her death and leaves the ledger with the one person who would be able to crack it. But given there's a diamond cartel on her ass, and whoever hired her is also looking for her, she splits the locations of the ledger and the cipher and pulls a Houdini."

"All the while she's made sure her resident code cracker has access to both pieces." Ariel's voice was tight.

"And Neela being Neela, she couldn't let the puzzle go. She had to keep picking at it. Keep trying to solve it. It's how her brain works. She won't let anything go until it makes sense to her. So basically, she ran off with the person who has possibly been trying to get at her this whole time."

"There's no way to know. And let's face it. Neela *wanted* to believe Willa, so there wasn't much you could do."

"You know, as bodyguards go, I might be shitty."

She snort-laughed. "Maybe. But I'm the one who told you your prime directive was the baby. Like Bipps, I thought the worse we'd deal with was a kidnap and ransom crew. Not a fucking diamond cartel."

I prayed that, like usual, Mayzie had Bunbun in her grip. If you tried to separate her from Bunbun, she would scream her bloody head off. I'd realized that on the first day and had a feeling that tracker might come in handy eventually. And it was a good thing I'd thought of it.

"I have them." She rattled off their location.

I'd grabbed my cache of ammo. I had no idea how many people I was going to have to fight. But there was no way I was letting Satorini keep her. It was my job to protect her. She'd become my own. And once I had her safe, I was going to go get her mother and bring her home safely too.

Jax...

LUCKILY, Mayzie was still on Lord's Island. The motherfucker who'd taken her had her stashed not even half a mile from the street I'd grown up on. Just outside of the city center, things went wilderness quiet.

I drove up to the quiet suburban house and parked down the street. Everything looked all nice and cozy. I took my tablet with me, trying to appear as normal as possible with my all-black getup and duffle full of enough weapons to arm a small militia.

I did two walk-bys at the house. From what I could see, there were four men. Two guards on watch outside, two inside. The ones outside, I could handle. What I didn't want to do was spook the crazies inside and have them hurt Mayzie in the crossfire, which meant I needed to be quiet and efficient. Good thing I had experience with that.

The first guard was easy. He had his back to me. One hand around his mouth, one arm around his neck, and I dragged him back just as I'd been taught during Special Forces training with the Winston Isles Army. I moved the body to the back bushes where he'dbe less conspicuous. But God only knew how long he'd stay that way. I needed to keep the body count low. I'd have to move quickly.

The other guard turned just as I was coming up on his back. He reached for his weapon, so I had to be a little less neat with that one, a little less clean. My knife sliced across his throat, spurting blood everywhere.

I moved the body over by the big oak to the side of the house. I hid it as best I could and then went for the door. There was a man in the kitchen with his back to me. "Hey, Phelps. Where the hell did you put the—" He turned around and froze, reaching for his weapon. I downed him with one bullet.

Head shot.

The problem was there was a lot of noise as he went down. Another voice called from inside, "What the fuck is going on in there? If this baby starts crying one more time, I will fucking feed you to her. She won't eat anything I give her."

"That's because she doesn't like regular baby food, you asshole." I couldn't help but be pleased that Mayzie was giving this motherfucker hell. He came around the corner of the kitchen, saw his idiot friend, and dove back around the corner. As he ran, I chased after him. *Fuck.*

I had to get to him before he got to Mayzie. I had to get him before... He turned around, gun aimed, but I fired first. The bullet hit him in the shoulder, and he went down.

"Who the fuck are you?"

"What? You and your friends shoot me in the goddamn chest and you don't recognize me?"

"You were dead."

"Well, it seems that rumors of my demise have been greatly exaggerated. You can thank your friend Willa for that one. She just said it to me two days ago."

The asshole's eyes went wide as my foot stepped on his arm that was leaking all over the place. "Who the fuck sent you, Santorini?"

He tried to dislodge my leg with his arm. But then I shot him in the other one too.

He bellowed. "Aargh. You son of a bitch."

"No, you shot me. I figure tit for tat. You shot me twice, I shot you twice. See how that goes?"

"Why did you come after us?"

I made it a point to dig my toe into his open wound. He yelled.

"You can yell all you want, but your friends aren't coming for you. Let me repeat myself. What do you want?"

"The girl."

"Willa?"

He hissed. "Fuck you."

"No thanks. I'm in love with someone else. Are you after Willa or Neela?"

He coughed and clawed at my foot. "The c-code breaker. It was Willa's plan."

I glowered at him. “So, you took Mayzie, for what, revenge?"

"Insurance. It's Willa. I'm here for the money. Don’t trust her."

I stared down at him. "You are the worst kind of fucktard twat. You don't even give a shit about the baby."

"I didn't want a baby."

"Why is it that the biggest assholes get the best shit? So what, are you planning to rob some very bad people?"

"It was Willa. She wanted the big score. Vanhorn kept notes of all the transactions. All the dirty money, cartels, bankers, Wall Street, and politicians. His whole list of clients is in that ledger. His bank account codes. Everything. We were going to take over."

"And you played Neela?"

He groaned. "I'm telling you it was Willa's plan. Give the bitch what she's always wanted, you know, someone to care about her, love her, make her more malleable and susceptible to helping us. It worked too. I was supposed to take the baby to force her to help."

Oh, my brave Neela. She was refusing to help, so Willa had kidnapped her own daughter.

"Thank you very much. You've been very helpful. Now, if you stay still, there is a chance that you might not bleed out. But if you move around too much, you could bleed to death. Totally up to you. I'm going to have to take the baby now."

I ran into the backroom where I heard Mayzie crying.

I found her on a bed, precariously leaning over the edge, trying to reach Bunbun. "Oh, baby girl."

She gave me a mournful wail when she saw me.

"I know. I know. Bunbun is down there." I grabbed her bunny and gave it to her, and she smiled at me and then clapped.

"Da?"

"Yeah, I'm here. Let's go get your mummy."

She clapped. "Ma."

"Yeah, I know. I miss her too."

I carried her out of that house and refused to look back at

any of them. Once I had Mayzie in the car, I called the police, let them know the address, and told them that I'd heard gun shots. Any luck and Satorini would still be alive and more than happy to spill the beans on Willa.

"Come on, Mayzie love. Let's go get your mama."

NINETEEN

NEELA...

STALL, *stall.*

I needed to stall for time. But now, Jax had woken up. If he was up, he'd have figured out what I'd done and called in the cavalry. And Ariel sure as shit would have asked Bex where I'd go.

"Jesus Christ, Willa. How did we end up here?"

"Look, I just always wanted more. I knew I was destined for more. There are people like you who are just happy to go along, but me, I knew I was supposed to be great. I knew how amazing I was supposed to be. And sometimes, money is an obstacle. So I removed that obstacle. You can't judge me for it."

"Why do you always think I'm desperate to judge you? I'm just trying to understand what you're going through and why you make the decisions that you make."

"You will never see me happy or satisfied with anything."

"You're always looking for the next thing. What you have is never enough. You were never happy. You always wanted what someone else had. I never understood that."

"You wouldn't understand. Why should I be happy with

scraps? Why should I be happy with what someone gives me? I know how amazing I could be. Why should I settle for anything less?"

"You're not settling well."

"Look, who cares how I got here? It's who I am, so deal with it."

I don't know what made me ask when I knew I wouldn't like the answer, but I asked nonetheless.

"What will happen at the end of this Willa? You get those names and buy your freedom or their silence with them?"

She frowned at me. "I want to be able to not have to look over my shoulder all the time. It's exhausting."

"You say that like you didn't do this to yourself."

"There you go judging again."

"Or you do damage to yourself. Your name is all over that ledger. Transactions, dates... this isn't some key that will break you out of your prison. You were a despised partner."

Her eyes went wide. "You deciphered it."

"Not all of it, but most of it. And I find you and what you've done horrible and exhausting. God, you must be tired."

Willa rubbed her arms. "You weren't supposed to have deciphered it yet. It was supposed to take you longer."

"Yeah well, chalk it up to me being a nerd with no friends, not even the ones you threw my way from your scraps. I spent a lot of time watching Star Trek."

Willa frowned. "Do you mind telling me what that means?"

I shook my head. "Give me the rest of the cipher."

She shook her head. "No, you're going to give me the ledger, and then you're going to tell me how to decipher it and what you've deciphered so far."

I shook my head. "No, I'm not. We're going to take it and forward it to the authorities."

She laughed. "Are you kidding me? I'll end up dead."

"You will not. You should have gone to the authorities yourself."

"Neela, if you do this, you will never see Mayzie again."

I wasn't dealing with her threats. She'd been threatening me since we were kids. "We're doing this my way. I'm not helping you with the damn thing. You're going to give me that cipher, and I'm going to give you to the police."

"Are you insane?" Willa's hands shook.

"Willa, this is really unnecessary."

"I'm sorry. This is not how this works. How this works is you'll give me the ledger, and then I'll use the cipher here to decode the rest of it. And then I'll leave. I already have bidders for the list of names. Then I'll grab my kid, and we'll ghost. Our property is all over the world. I'll never have to worry about what I'll do for money."

"Oh, I see you're still delusional. No. The answer is no."

With a screech, Willa raised her arms as if she was going to club me with the gun. I slid my hands quickly up to the front of my face and deflected her arms. She shouted, "I want what's mine."

"Well, unless you're going to use nice words, it's not coming. It's not happening for you."

She disengaged the safety. "If you fuck with me, you're going to end up dead. Now, where is the goddamn ledger?"

"If you kill me, you're never going to find out. So, we're just at a stalemate, right?"

"I hate you. I have always hated you."

Just hearing her say the words and know I'd been right

didn't bring me comfort. But at least I knew I hadn't made it up in my mind. Over the years she *had* truly hated me. "Well, that's nice to know."

She tried to hit me again. This time, I took the brunt on my jaw and my head snapped to the side. I fought my darkening vision and stayed upright. "I don't know what I ever did to make you hate me so much."

"You came from a goddamn perfect family. Yeah, your mom died. But your dad, he loved you. He taught you things and spent time with you. All you ever did was whine about how your mother died. And then your father died. I was so jealous of you."

"I don't know why you were jealous of me."

Willa raised her arms again, and this time, I ducked to avoid her. "You, come here."

"You hitting me isn't going to get you what you want."

"No, but it will give me some goddamn satisfaction. God, you even had to have the hot guy."

"Why do you begrudge me having something? Why? That's not how love works Willa."

"Well, you had someone to teach you. I never had that person."

"I would have done it. I would have taught you mercy and compassion."

"You're so full of yourself. I wish, we'd never taken you in." She reached for me again, and I stayed just out of range.

She raised the gun at me again and I knew. She had absolutely gone off the rails and she would absolutely kill me. She'd stopped caring about having me decipher the ledger. Instead her anger and hate had taken over.

If I didn't do something she was going to kill me. I was

dumb. I knew. The odds were slim, but I wasn't going to take this lying down. I'd had plenty of that my whole life.

I lunged for her, grabbing for the gun. No way was I letting her shoot me and no way was she letting me have the gun, so it was one hell of a fight. She fought my grip, I pushed her back. If this was how it was going to end, at least I wasn't taking it lying down.

With grunts and heaves, we wrestled the gun between our bodies and I met her gaze. "Do not do this, Willa."

"I wouldn't have to if you just gave me what I wanted."

Then the ear-splitting crack reverberated between us and I winced as my stomach roiled. Was I hit? I waited for the pain, but none came.

"I will kill you," she growled at me.

But I managed to squeeze that tender spot in her wrist just so and she dropped the gun. Then, I did the one thing I've been dying to do since she turned up on my doorstep. I faced her. "You almost shot me? After everything?" Hand raised, palm closed, I hit her in the face.

Petty? Maybe. But goddamn satisfying. It was only after I watched dispassionately as her head snapped back that I realized she'd shot herself...in the foot. Literally and figuratively. Shit.

I whipped off my jacket as she slumped to the ground. I had no choice but to apply pressure to her foot. She might hate me and have tried to kill me, but, I wasn't going to let her die. She was still Mayzie's mom.

The doors to the yoga studio busted open, and Ariel, Tamsin, and Jameson came in. "Jesus Christ. What are you guys doing here?"

Ariel stared at me. "Jax called. We didn't find you at the ferry."

"We took a charter boat. And Willa and I needed to have it out. I wanted to see how much she hated me before deciding what to do with her. She's all yours. Here is the secondary cipher. Those embossed symbols on the edges of the authentic ledger, and the markings, those are names. And I'm pretty sure she'll be more than happy to give them to you. I, for one, just need to find my guy."

Ariel smiled at me. "Pretty bad ass, Neela."

"I'm not. But when I channel Jax, I come pretty damn near close. Now, does one of you know how to staunch bleeding?"

Jax...

I CRADLED Mayzie to my chest. Now that the adrenaline was wearing off, I could feel my bones trying to crack and realign. I was feeling foggy from the drugs they'd injected me with. Just on the edges, but enough to feel off. And my heart, the worry constricting it, I needed to get to Neela. I needed to keep her safe.

You failed her. You let her go off with the enemy.

Even though I'd suspected what Willa was, I'd still let my guard down. That was dumb. But Neela was stubborn. Mule-headed. Refused to listen to reason.

I wonder why that is?

She hated being told what to do, and I was used to being in charge. We'd have to work on that.

Once the ferry had landed on the main island, I wasted no

time. Trace was there with the car. I unstrapped the baby and handed her over to him. "Put her in the back."

He didn't even argue, which told me there was trouble.

"Neela. What does the GPS say?"

Trace strapped Mayzie in and then climbed into the passenger seat next to me.

"Relax. Ariel's already on her way to her."

"I will not fucking relax until I know she's okay."

Trace wasn't even buckled in when I kicked the car into gear. He would just have to hold on, because I needed to get to her.

At that time of night, the streets around the main shopping district were quiet as church mice. Eerily silent. Nothing was open that late. No reason for anything to be open.

The surrounding streets with all the restaurants were still semi-alive, but the area where we were was dead.

We turned the corner though, and things weren't dead anymore. There were cop cars everywhere.

What little adrenaline I had left in my body surged back, and my heart hammered. I barely even threw the car into park before I tried to climb out.

"Jax, it's fine. She's fine."

"Shut up."

I ran for the cars.

One of the patrol cops looked like he wanted to try his luck at stopping me from going inside.

I gave him a shake of my head. "You don't want to try this."

He frowned, and his hand went to his gun. I cursed under my breath and put my hands up. "That's my girlfriend in there. I need to see her."

He put his hand up. "Sir, you can't go inside. There's been a shooting."

"I know."

And then I remembered my Royal Elite badge.

I pulled it out and flashed it. He frowned, shook his head then he let me pass.

Holy hell. If I'd known that badge would get me in and out of trouble, I'd have been using it a lot more often.

I ran past the tape. Past those filing around.

Inside, I followed the crowd, eyes scanning for her. *Oh God, please let her be alive. Please, please, please fucking let her be alive.*

I saw Ariel first. Her gaze was grim. "Jax. Listen before you go in there—"

I wasn't listening. I barged past her. "Neela? Neela!"

I shoved past the policeman at the door to the women's bathroom. "Neela."

From the corner, her voice was calm. "Jax."

I whipped around. "Oh my God."

She was covered in blood. "I will kill her."

"It's unnecessary. I'm fine. I'm fine."

My hands were gentle on her face. When she winced, I wanted to pull back, but I had to check her. Make sure she wasn't seriously hurt.

"I woke up and you weren't there. You were gone. And God I could have killed you myself. You were reckless and stubborn."

"I'm sorry. I just knew you wouldn't me let go. And I knew I had to do it. No way Willa was going to do things the right way. She would have found a way to kill us first. And I was the one she wanted, so I took her away from you and Mayzie. I'm sorry."

" Why would you do that to me? Don't you know how much I love you?"

"I am so, so sorry. But Willa said it herself. Mayzie was your job. Not me. I wanted to do what I could."

Her lips quivered. I pulled her in, wrapping my arms around her, and only then was I able to breathe. Only then could I relax. She was safe. She was in my arms. She was breathing. She was okay. Her arms shook as they wrapped around me. "I'm sorry. I'm so sorry. I know." And then she pulled back. "Mayzie, where's Mayzie?"

I couldn't help it, the smile tightening my lips. This is what a mother should do. A mother should worry about her child, how she was doing, how she was fairing. Willa never worried.

"She's fine. I promise. She had an unforeseen adventure, but I got her. I promise you she's okay."

She frowned. I could tell she wanted to ask all the questions, but I couldn't answer them right then. I just needed to hold her, heal her. Confirm for myself that she was alive.

"Let's go."

She nodded. "Yeah. I just want to see Mayzie."

It only then occurred to me to ask, "Where's Willa?"

She inhaled deeply and sighed. "She's been arrested. She tried to kill me. She was pissed I didn't bring her the authentic ledger."

"You bluffed her?"

"Not exactly a bluff. I did have the ledger. Just not the way she wanted it. It was a copy. The embossed pages with the secondary code didn't come through on the printout. They were only in the original. And to get the original meant going to Ariel."

"She tried to kill you?" I ground my teeth together. "Where the fuck is she?"

Neela held on tight to my biceps. "Stop. I'm safe. Okay? I remembered how to look after myself. I'm okay. I promise."

I stared at her. "Never again, okay?"

She nodded. "I promise."

"Let's get out of here."

Ariel was waiting for us in the hallway.

"Jax, you need to let Neela get checked out."

I shook my head. "The hell I will. I'll take her to the hospital myself."

Ariel sighed. "The both of you actually need to get checked out. But she looks more urgent. Let's get the cuts and bruises cleaned. And then you can take her to the hospital, okay? The EMTs are outside."

I glowered at Ariel. But I knew what she wanted. To speak to me privately for a moment. I squeezed Neela tight and kissed her forehead. "I'll be right there."

She nodded. And as she passed Ariel, Ariel took her hand and squeezed. "You did great."

I watched as Neela limped outside, not needing my support, not needing anyone. She had taken care of the bad guy all by herself. Ariel met my gaze. "She's a tough cookie."

"She is mule-headed. She fucking drugged me so she could sneak away and protect me and Mayzie."

Ariel shook her head. "Yeah, that sounds like something you would do."

"It's insane. She could have been killed. And then stupid Satorini was part of Willa's plan all along. She planned to manipulate Neela into helping her, and then while I was down for the count, he came and took the baby."

Ariel's sighed. "Christ this was such a shit show. Do I have bodies to clean up?"

"Taken care of. I'll debrief you in the morning. But yeah, basically. Satorini and his men came in. They took Mayzie and shot me. When I came to, I went after her."

"You need a medic?" Ariel ran her hands through her hair. "This is the worst."

"No, the vest caught the bullets. But I want Mayzie checked."

"Nice work on tracking the baby by the way."

I shrugged. "Mr. Bunbun. She won't go anywhere without the damn thing. And if she's not holding it, she's screaming about holding it. So I figured outside implanting a GPS tracker under her skin, which, you know, unethical, planting a tracker in him was the easiest way to track her. I didn't trust Willa."

"Jesus." She shook her head. "I don't know how you pulled it off, but you did."

"Actually, I failed. I only protected the baby. I failed to protect Neela."

"Remember, the baby was your assignment, not the mother."

"Yeah, well, package deal."

"You okay? You look a little rough around the edges."

"Nothing that some uninterrupted sleep and maybe unwrapping my ribs won't solve."

"Are they broken or just bruised?"

"I didn't break them so much as they were broken for me. Close range shots to the chest will do that, but luckily that's the worst of it."

She rolled her eyes. "Semantics. All right. Let's get you checked out."

"Yup, point me in the direction of Neela's ambulance."

"You really love her, don't you?"

"Yup. It's the last thing I wanted. Honestly I did try to follow the rules."

"Yeah, I saw. There really was no stopping it, was there?"

I grinned at her. "Nope."

"Well, in that case, I guess you guys will figure out the whole Royal Guard thing."

I stared at her. "Are you serious?"

She nodded. "I heard from Ethan tonight before all hell broke loose. He's giving you tenure you earned before leaving the guard. He'll modify your paperwork to say you were on sabbatical."

My jaw unhinged. "It wasn't exactly a sabbatical."

She shrugged. "It's been less than a year. You came back. Sometimes you fudge some stuff to make things work, to make things right."

"So I'm back in."

She nodded. "Yeah. Congratulations. You did a great job."

I frowned though. "But what about you?"

Her lips ticked up at the corner. "Aw, don't tell me you've gotten used to me now. I was kind of relishing being a pain in your ass."

"Well, you still are a pain in my ass. But we were building something."

"Yeah, we were. I'll miss you, but I knew this was what you wanted. This was the goal all along. Enjoy it."

She went to handle the police. I went toward Neela. But as I approached the woman that I loved, I tried to figure out how the hell I was going to tell her that I was going back into the Royal Guard. I knew that wasn't the kind of lifestyle she wanted. She'd been really clear. She'd grown up around that all her life.

Constant monitoring, constantly having protection around. She didn't want that. She didn't want that for Mayzie. Was I going to lose her?

The pit fell out of the bottom of my stomach. I couldn't lose her. Not after everything we'd been through.

She glanced up from where one of the techs was tending to a cut on her forehead. Her smile was so sweet, so genuine.

For one more night, I'd enjoy that. I'd just hold her. Tomorrow, tomorrow I would tell her that I was going back to the Guard.

TWENTY

Neela…

He was off. Something was wrong. I didn't know what exactly, but I could tell. I just feel that he was on edge. He was still attempting to wrap himself around me like a giant piece of bubble wrap every chance he got since we'd been home. He'd been mum. I still didn't know what any of this meant. All I knew was I wanted him. I wanted Mayzie.

Willa was going to jail. Mr. Bipps had already called to inform me that, as Willa was alive, the authorities had also tacked on fraud as one of her charges. There were so many.

The one unexpected thing was that Mayzie still needed a guardian. And as I'd been the one to watch over her, if I wanted I could still be her guardian. Willa being alive meant there were a lot of changes though. There would no longer need to be an executor of Willa's estate, and the government was seizing most of it anyway, so we wouldn't be staying in the house much longer. I knew that much. They would take away the only home Mayzie knew. And of course, Jax would be going too because we no longer needed bodyguards. No one was trying to kill us anymore.

"Talk to me, Jax."

He kissed my ear as we lay on the couch. Mayzie was in her playpen, quietly banging things and gnawing on the foot of Mr. Ta.

"I am talking to you. If you like, I can put Mayzie to bed and we can talk some more."

Despite my mood, I giggled. "Jesus, I don't know how you can keep going. My muscles are mush, complete mush, from you making me have too many orgasms."

"There's no such thing as too many orgasms. Here, I'll show you."

His hand slid down my belly and played with the edge of my panties.

"Jax. Mayzie."

"She's sitting in a playpen. She can't see a thing."

His fingers traversed past the elastic, and I could feel it again, the quick build, the desperate, clawing need for him. God, it was just so easy with him. He was all I wanted. All the time.

But you can't have him.

I clamped my hand around his wrist, stopping him.

His hand stilled. "What's wrong? Are you sore?"

I shook my head. "No. I'm not sore. I'm used to your size by now."

He chuckled. "I guess that's good?"

"Yeah, it's good. But we can't."

He pulled his hand back but kept it tucked around my belly. "Tell me what's wrong?"

I rolled in his arms and met his gaze. "You tell me. Something's off with you. I know it. You know it. So just tell me."

"I'd rather just stay in this cocoon for a while longer."

"I know. But that isn't reality. In a couple days I'm going to have to take Mayzie out of here. Find a flat or a small house somewhere, and I'm going to raise her."

"Mr. Bipps said they were only seizing Willa's assets, not Mayzie's. Mayzie has been a tax paying citizen her whole life, even though she's only a year old. So we're using the money that's squirreled away. We'll get something nice. Quiet. Normal."

"I want nothing more than to spend time with you being normal. But please tell me what's wrong. I can't stand that you're not telling me something."

He sighed. "I've been offered my post back in the Royal Guard."

I startled. " You actually want to *return* to the Royal Guard?"

"Yeah."

I couldn't help it, I tried to shelter myself against whatever else he was going to tell me, but he wouldn't let me go. He just kept his arms wrapped around me and held me tight.

"This doesn't change anything. It just means I'll work for someone else. And I know you have the whole men-in-black problem, but this is what I was meant to do."

He thought I would stop him from what he was meant to do? "Jax, I want for you what *you* want."

His brows lifted. "You do?"

"Yes, I do. But you took the job already?"

"Yeah. I mean that was kind of the whole purpose of why I was here."

Now I really pulled back and sat up. "Wait, you don't really work for Ariel?"

He sat up too and ran his hands through his hair. "Okay, look, it's complicated. I did work for Ariel. I mean technically, I still do until next week."

"Next week? You've got to go back to the Guard next week?"

He nodded. "Yeah. I mean I'll go in, do paperwork and all that, and it'll take another week for an assignment."

"So just like that, we're done."

He glowered at me. "No. We're not done. You and I and Mayzie. We are family."

I shook my head. "How are we a family when you won't even tell me what you really do, who you really are, and then you're off on some adventure without even talking to me about it? Newsflash, I want what you want. If you want to be in the Royal Guard, I'll find a way to be okay with that. I'll do what you want, but Jesus, you just took the job and didn't even talk to me. What are we even doing?"

"We're a family. You, me, and Mayzie."

"No. Apparently, we're not family. You were my bodyguard, I guess, and her nanny. We aren't family. The Guard, that's your real family, isn't it?"

He opened his jaw, and then he snapped it shut.

"Jesus, all the time you were talking about how you were trying to get back to family, you were talking about that."

"Please don't be upset. I know how you grew up. The contracts your father worked on were volatile, and he needed guards. And I know you didn't feel safe, but what I do is different."

"You think this is about that? You just decided you were going back to the Guard. *You didn't talk to me about it.* You didn't communicate anything with me you just... That was just your plan and you never said a word."

"Jesus, it's been the plan. I just... We never really had a chance to talk about it."

"You're right. We didn't. Because at the end of the day, I guess we didn't really know each other that well."

He frowned. "No, don't say that. Don't do that. You know me better than anyone else in the world. You and Mayzie *are* my family. I just always wanted to be able to return to the Royal Guard."

"Then I'm glad for you. I am. You should have what you want, and I wouldn't want to stop you from that. But you're going to have to talk to us... to me. When you don't, I feel like I don't matter, like I'm being overlooked again. You had your whole life planned out, and it didn't include the two of us, which is fine. Mayzie and I will be okay on our own."

I stood up, grabbed Mayzie, and headed up the stairs. I didn't look back at him.

Jax...

I DIDN'T KNOW where I fucked up. One moment, everything was good. We were all happy. But she was right. I'd had my own goal, and there was no backing away from it. But it wasn't like I couldn't include her.

You can't move a baby into Guard quarters.

No, but I get off the palace grounds enough. I could see them. Besides not all guards lived on the grounds.

But you're just coming back. It would be better if you were on palace grounds.

I met Roone at the same pub as last time.

He stood and gave me a grin when I walked through the front door. "Mate, glad to see your sorry face."

I grinned. "You too, you knob."

He signaled for the waitress to bring me a drink, and then he grinned at me. "Told you Ariel was a miracle worker."

"Yeah. I didn't actually think she'd pull it off, but she clearly did."

Roone frowned at me. "Why don't you look happy?"

"No, I am. I just... I didn't... I guess part of me didn't expect it to happen."

"Why not? From my experience, when that one says she's going to do something, she does it. You may not like it, but it's going to get done."

I nodded slowly. "Yeah, I know, I know. And it is what I want. That was the goal. Get back into the Guard. I owe Ethan a case of scotch or something."

Roone studied me. "You look happy but not happy. What's wrong?"

"It's fine. It's just Neela."

Roone grinned. "Ah, so you fell in love with the client."

"You say that like it's completely normal."

"Well, it kind of is. Happens a lot... To the best of us. So, you fell in love. What's the problem?"

"Well, it's not just Neela. It's Mayzie too, and I can't exactly put an active one-year-old in Guard housing."

He frowned. "Okay, you have a point there. But you could have them over often."

"Come on. You know how that goes. I gotta work here, I gotta work there. It doesn't mesh."

"Come on, lots of guards have families."

"Yeah, the more settled guys. Ethan took me off 'sabbatical,' but I saw the terms of the contract. I'll need to be on site."

Roone frowned. "Are you considering not taking it?"

"No. That's non-negotiable. Of course, I'm taking it."

Are you?

"I just have to figure out the Neela and Mayzie thing.

Roone nodded slowly. "You know, I get it. Sometimes you think you want one thing. And then you get it, and you realize that the thing you wanted is not at all what you thought. Or things change. It's not the end of the world, man."

"I want to be part of the Guard again. I just... I also want my family."

Roone studied me. "Look mate, I get it. Trust me, I do. Love can be tricky. I also know what it's like to think you have to give something up. I went through it with Jessa. I thought I wasn't good enough, thought Sebastian would be pissed that I was shagging his sister."

"Hell, I'd be pissed if you were shagging my sister, and I like you."

Roone just rolled his eyes, ignoring me. "My point is that whatever had happened, I knew I couldn't live without her. Whether that meant I was in the Guard or I had to quit to go live with her in London and be her personal bitch or whatever, I had to do it. I needed her. She was... she *is* everything. So I get it. You just think about what your priorities are and what you can and can't live without."

I ran a hand over my face. I knew the answer to that. It was easy, automatic. I couldn't live without Neela or Mayzie. "Love is a bitch, man."

Roone grinned. "Oh yeah. Did you think that shit would be easy?"

"It would be really fucking helpful if it was."

"Here's the kicker of it. She loves you, so she'll want you to do the thing that makes you happy. She'll just want you to be communicative about it."

I winced.

Roone chuckled. "Oh, you didn't tell her about it until you'd already made your choice?"

I winced again.

"Mate, the number one way to piss a woman off is to leave her out of the decision-making process. It makes her feel irrelevant, unneeded."

"Yeah, I see that now. I just... it was everything I wanted, so I had to say yes. I didn't even think about talking to her first."

Roone took a sip of his beer. "Yeah, mate, talk to her. I mean, isn't it easier when you talk shit out anyway? You talk through it and have someone else to bounce shit off of. You don't have to be stuck in your own idiotic head all the time."

"Yeah, when you put it like that, it makes sense."

"Talk to her. That generally solves about 97 percent of these issues. The job is yours if you want it. And if you don't want it, I'm pretty sure Ariel would be happy to keep you on her team."

"Yeah, well, I kept a baby alive."

Roone grinned. "You'd be surprised how difficult that can be."

"Tell me about it."

TWENTY-ONE

NEELA...

JUST BECAUSE I'D come to the party didn't mean I wasn't still pissed as hell at Jax. But Ariel and the rest of the team had become family to us. Besides, Bex insisted I come.

Mostly, she wanted to ogle Trace. Adam was still working his awful flirting so at least they were happy. And Mayzie, well, she had been missing Jax. We still had some security in case there were any of Vanhorn's men left with a grudge, but no Jax as we couldn't see eye to eye.

I missed him. More than I thought I could miss someone. Granted life before him and Mayzie was like a shadow life. I had no clue about the depths of love until I fell for the both of them.

So much had changed in the month Jax had come to live with me and so much more had changed in the last few weeks since we'd been back.

As far as Mayzie was concerned, Michael Satorini signed away his parental rights. Ariel suspected he had some hidden wealth he wanted untouched while he was in prison. He wasn't exactly the sharing type.

As for Willa, she was going to be in jail for a long time. Her lawyer had approached me to speak as a character witness. He'd tried to work the 'Willa wasn't in her right mind' angle. Tried to make it seem she was afraid for her life and that affected her decision making.

I could actually see that. She had certainly been scared. But her own decisions led to her situation, so there was not much to be done about it.

And she tried to kill you.

Yeah, there was that.

Willa was facing charges for fraud for her faked death, attempted murder and kidnapping of me, fraud for her shady dealings, trafficking stolen good, and money laundering. It was going to be a long time before she saw the light of day.

Trace came for Mayzie first. She was happy to have cuddles, but she kept looking around. I knew she wanted Jax, but I didn't see him right away. It was Ariel who approached me with champagne. "Hi you."

"Hey, Ariel."

"Whenever you're ready for a gig on the Royal Elite team, you let me know. You were just as badass as any of us."

"Thank you, but I am really looking forward to finding a new normal, you know, without people trying to kill me every other day."

Ariel rolled her eyes. "God, imagine the boredom," she said, chuckling.

"Right?"

"But seriously. You have nothing to worry about. The additional security is just until we wrangle up the last couple of Vanhorn's associates. With what you and your team deciphered from his ledger, the ramifications are widespread, not just in the islands. Corruption, international espionage, drugs, politics. The Winston Isles Bureau of Investigation and Interpol will be unwinding that network for years. But what you and your team did, decoding the ledger, is a huge deal. You'll probably be fielding job offers."

"It's already started." The phone hadn't stopped ringing since we turned in that ledger. We were turning down work, it was so crazy. Richard had called too, but given what Bex had said to him, I doubted he'd ever be calling again.

"You look beautiful."

A shiver danced over my spine at the sound of his voice. It took everything I had not to turn and leap into his arms. Instead I turned slowly around. "Jax."

Suddenly everyone became very busy and let us be. "I—"

"Please don't." I shook my head. "I don't think my heart can break anymore."

"Then stop breaking it yourself and just listen to me. I'm not taking the job."

Idiot. I swear I was going to kill him. Why couldn't he see that it wasn't about the job. It was about him shutting me out. "That's not at all what I wanted."

"I know. If you let me, I'd love to tell you why."

I lifted my chin to meet his gaze, brushing my hair over my shoulder. "Fine."

"I fucked up. I thought I could just control every situation, and when I did that, the only thing that ever mattered to me went tits up."

"Is that the official term?"

"Yeah. It is. I was a twat. Plain and simple. I didn't even consider talking to you. It was just the goal and I didn't think.

But I had to examine it when I had the thing I said I wanted, but I still wasn't happy."

My eyes stung, but I refused to cry.

"You and Mayzie have become my whole world. You are my family. You are the ones who brought me back to life. I should never have discounted that. The only excuse I have is that love bloody broadsided me, and I wasn't ready. It wasn't in the plan. All that was supposed to happen was I was supposed to protect the heiress, instead, I fell in love with the both of you."

"Jax..." *Shit.* I could feel the impending tears.

"I love you. I want you by my side and Mayzie on my shoulders giggling like a loon."

"Is this real?" my voice shook as I spoke.

Jax grinned. "I'm so glad you asked that." He wrapped his arms around me and picked me up. "It is real. And as soon as Mayzie is big enough to make it all the way down the aisle, I'm going to ask you to marry me."

I swiped at one of the escaped tears. "I love you so much."

"I know. I'm remarkably good looking."

I rolled my eyes. "Yes, you are. And bossy too."

"I have it on good authority you like bossy." He dipped his head, angling slightly. The kiss he gave me was both sweet and potent, and my head spun.

But just before I could demand he take me somewhere private with a flat surface, he pulled back. "Now where is our daughter? I owe her a kiss too."

Jax...

I SAT BACK and watched as Trace played with Mayzie. That little traitor had ditched me for him because he had a beard. She laughed as she tugged it, and I was pretty sure that asshole wore the scruff on purpose just so she would have something to pull.

Trace slid me a glance and grinned. "Don't be jealous just because you can't grow facial hair."

"I can grow facial hair just fine," I muttered. "It just happens to be that Neela prefers me without it."

Neela wrinkled her face. "Too scratchy."

Trace winked at her. "Scratchy can be fun."

Ariel, Jameson, Tamsin, and Zia all groaned from the kitchen. "Eeeww."

Ariel came out with the bread and a bread knife.

Zia came out with the sauce, and Jameson had the pasta. Tamsin followed with a bottle of wine.

Neela perked up. "Oh my God. I swear you should let me help."

Ariel shook her head. "Nope. Rule is, family cooks, family serves."

"But aren't I family now?"

Ariel grinned at that. "Yes, you are, because someone here can't follow the damn rules. But you're not on the payroll, so you sit."

Yeah, there was still that matter, which I knew we were going to have to discuss at some point. But I'd already made a decision about what I wanted out of my life, and surprisingly, it was right there in the room with me. These peoplewho had become my team, these people who had saved me.

Three months ago, I was living a completely different life, wondering what the hell happened to me. One call, one run in with Ariel, and I had the kind of life I'd always wanted.

Family that was mine, a woman I could love, and a future. The Guard also held a certain kind of future. One I would love, but it would take away a chance at a lot more.

If I went back in, I'd have to be a rookie again, and I would be travelling all the time. The more coveted roles where you get to stay at home and have a family were assigned to those with seniority and in the higher-up positions. But I knew I could have that by being here at Royal Elite. Besides, Ariel, Trace, Jameson, Zia, Tamsin, and myself had built something important, and I wasn't ready to walk away from that yet. Royal Elite felt like more than family.

One second, we were all laughing and enjoying our beers. The next, we all palmed our weapons and took defensive positions.

Ariel came back out of the kitchen and rolled her eyes. "I'm glad to see you guys all have the right instincts, but relax. They were invited."

What the hell did she mean *they* were invited? We were all present.

And then she opened the door. All of us except Ariel and Mayzie fell to one knee.

Jesus, the fucking royals were joining us for dinner? I suddenly rethought my choice of jeans.

The king was quick to dismiss formalities though. "Jesus, all of you up. None of that. Someone told me this was a family dinner."

Family... the king... *holy shit.*

We were all, admittedly, a little stiff at first, but the queen, who insisted we all just call her Penny, was quick to break the ice.

Before I knew it, we were having dinner with royalty. Trace

was fighting with Prince Lucas over who was a better basketball team, LA or the Warriors, and Sebastian was telling stories about Zia in the military.

Ariel caught me on the balcony. "You enjoying yourself?"

I grinned. "Yeah. Thank you for inviting Neela's team. I don't think Bex would have ever survived if she found out she didn't meet the king and queen. She's well chuffed."

"Well, we're all family now. Even though you'll be leaving me soon."

"Actually, about that..."

She raised a brow. "What do you mean?"

"Well, I think maybe I like *this* family team more. And staying here means being around as much as possible for Mayzie."

I could tell she was biting back a grin as she nodded. "Well, I mean, that's your choice, obviously. It's a difficult one to come to. Does it have anything to do with her?" Ariel inclined her head toward the living room where Neela held Mayzie asleep in her arms.

"It has a lot to do with both of them, actually. I made the dumb choice to leave the Guard last time because I thought leaving would preserve my idea of a family. But this... Royal Elite is a family too. And certainly, Neela and Mayzie are."

"Well, I think you and Neela are the best ones to give Mayzie stability. Even if Satorini is Mayzie's father, first of all, he's never getting out of jail. Second of all, never is he ever going to get custody of that baby."

"Good, because she's mine."

Ariel gave me one nod. "Okay, as long as you want to be here, I've got a spot for you. I do have a soft spot for British boys."

I headed back inside and found Neela. She gave me a broad grin. "Hey, there you are. What were you and Ariel talking about?"

"Oh, we were talking about my future."

"Oh, is that so?"

"Sure is."

"Are you going to tell me?"

I shrugged. "Maybe."

"Jax. Don't be such a guy. Spill."

"So, about the guard, the thing is the Guard would require me to be on the travelling team, which means I'd be away from my family too long."

She shook her head. "Oh my God, we would make it work. It's your dream to go back. Youhave been fighting for this. Mayzie and I will survive. We'll come up with a great schedule. Bex and Adam can handle so many little cases. I'll just take the larger ones. We'll get a team. And maybe I'll actually hire an actual nanny this time."

"You would do that?"

She grinned. "Of course. I love you. I love Mayzie. If we're going to be a family now, we'll make it work. You give up way too easily."

I shook my head. "No. I'm never giving up on you, ever. Besides, I like working for Royal Elite. As bosses go, Ariel is great, and there's no politics here. And there's more flexibility."

"Don't you dare give up your happiness for me and the baby. We wouldn't want that."

"I'm not giving up my happiness. Have you ever seen me this happy before?"

"Yes. After sex."

She said it so dead pan, a bark of laughter tore out of my chest, startling Mayzie. "Oh my God."

"Am I wrong?"

"No, no, not wrong. Just... I can't believe you said that."

"Yeah well, it's true."

"You're impossible."

"Am I? You can just call me right if you want."

"Yes, you are right. But I love you, and all I want to do is be with you all the time."

"Great. Whatever you do, I do too. We're a team. You, me, and Mayzie here. And the rest of the Royal Elite team."

She looked over to the side, and Trace winked at her. The idiot had been eavesdropping. "So, if you're staying on the Royal Elite team, that's great too. Whatever makes you happy..."

"You are what makes me happy." I leaned forward and gave her a kiss. Mayzie stirred in her arms and blinked up sleepily. "Da."

"See, she's trying to say Daddy."

Neela laughed. "Or, she's trying to say dog, or door. It's hard to tell with this kid."

"I'm telling you, it's daddy."

"Okay, whatever you need to believe."

Good thing I would have all the time in the world to prove I was right.

TWENTY-TWO

Ariel...

"You just had to make a show of it, didn't you?"

Sebastian chuckled low as he prowled around my office. "Well, if you're going to do something, do it right."

"You know you could have just requested us to come up," I said.

"I could've. But I wanted to come down to see you. I'm not going to sit on the throne and make subjects come to me. That's stupid."

I laughed. "Um, that's kind of what kings do."

He shook his head, brows dipping a little. "Not this king. Besides, I wanted to check in on you and see how you were doing."

"You could've called."

"You know full well I wasn't just going to call. You're a part of my family."

My face heated at that. "Aw shucks, my liege, are we gonna hug and stuff now?"

"I know how you feel about touching."

"I keep telling you, if we weren't a throuple, I'd be okay with it."

Sebastian just rolled his eyes. "As hot as I think watching you and Penny having sex would be, I don't think so. I'm not very good at sharing."

"Your loss then."

I'd been teasing him mercilessly for a long time about how he, Penny, and I were already in a relationship and he just needed to climb on board. While the banter was all in good fun, I was hyper-aware that everyone was outside my office doing the small-talk, dinner-party thing while Sebastian needed to talk to me about something important. "Spill. What do you need?"

He blinked rapidly. "What do you mean? I'm just catching up with you."

"Behind closed doors. So far you haven't said anything you couldn't have said out there. But you asked to speak to me privately, so that means something important is happening. You know I'm not good with small talk."

"Yeah, I haven't forgotten. Are you going to have a seat for this?"

I shook my head. "My office. So I'd rather you just spill it if you have something crazy to tell me like I'm no longer welcome at the palace or something."

He sighed, and my gut clenched. "Is that the fear you live with now?"

I tilted my chin up. "Yes, it's the fear I live with now. You are well within your rights to ban me from the palace. You are well within your rights to ban me from seeing Penny. You can do anything you want. You're the king now."

"I cannot do anything I want because I never would have let

you go. I have people I answer to, and you know it. If I had my way, you'd be back in the palace like you want."

I watched him warily. "What's going on? You're making me really nervous."

"As you know, I've been looking for a way around the Council. Looking for a way to make things work. I don't like that the Council has full control over my Royal Guard. I don't trust them... at least not all of them."

"Good. After what happened, you shouldn't trust everyone."

"Right. Anyway, I've been giving this a lot of thought, and I found a loophole."

"Loophole?"

"Yeah. I don't know if you remember from the history books, but there used to be King's Knights."

I frowned. "Yeah, like, when our grandparents were around? Maybe great-grandparents? I don't remember. It was certainly a while ago."

"Not anymore."

My eyes went wide. "Sebastian, what did you do?"

"I made you a Knight."

I wasn't sure if I should laugh, or cry, or warn him against poking the bear. "You did what?"

"The loophole was clear. Any monarch may create his own personal guard. For generations now, we've just gone with the Royal Guard. But since the Council is being so specific to the letter about who can and cannot guard us, companies like Royal Elite and Blake Security aren't an option for the royal family anymore. Even though during my father's time, it wasn't a problem."

"Well, it isn't your father's time now, is it?" I added softly.

"No, it certainly isn't. But because of everything that's happened in the last few years, the Council is trying to do everything by the letter. The hard letter. So I'm trying to find ways around them. You found a loophole for your boy Jax out there, and I found a loophole for you if you want it."

My heart skipped, stumbling over itself, trying to catch back up to its normal rhythm. "You want to make me a Knight?"

He grinned. "Yes, but not just you. Everyone who works for you."

"You're creating Knights."

He chuckled softly. "I think I just said that."

"Holy shit."

Sebastian grinned. "I know, right? Penny got all 'Knights of the Round Table' and shit about it."

"The Council's going to be gunning for you now."

"Well, they can try. They seem to forget I was pretty good at history. Not good enough to be an excellent historian, but I plan to find every single loophole I can exploit in my favor. Every single one. I've been sitting on the sidelines too long. And we've watched too many people get hurt and die because of it. It's time we go on the offensive. What do you say? Will you arise a Knight?"

"I mean if you insist. What will my title be?"

He grinned. "*Lady* Ariel Scott."

I scrunched my nose. "You couldn't come up with anything better than 'Lady'?"

"I know. But I wanted to stick to the letter of the Knighthood. At least for now. Once it's more established and around for a while, I can make some modifications."

I nodded. "That's unbelievable." And because I knew how

important and how significant this honor was, I added, "Your Majesty."

He slid a glance over to the glass doors to everyone settling in for a game of Mafia. "So, what do you say? You want to go tell the troops that they're going to have an all-access pass to the palace?"

"They're going to lose their shit."

"Probably. But it'll be good news, right?"

I grinned at him. "Uh, yeah. I think it'll be good news. So how does this work though? Will you direct us?"

Sebastian shook his head. "Yes, and no. It'll allow you full access to the palace whenever you want, your own entrance and everything. But mostly, you'll still be you, just doing your regular job. Unless I need you specifically to watch over someone, of course."

"I can't believe this."

He grinned. "I should be given an award or something. I've finally managed to render you speechless. It'll be great to have you roaming the halls of the palace again."

"Well, I mean it's not like I was banned."

"I know. But now you'll know you *belong* there. And you won't have to wear that stupid visitor's badge. It just looked wrong on you."

"I know, right? It totally clashed with my hair."

"Come on, Lady Ariel. Let's go make some Knights."

Ariel...

SIX MONTHS AGO, I'd had to start from scratch. With a little help from my family, I'd been able to build new purpose in my life.

I'd never have been able to pull it off without them. And I could never say *thank you* enough. Royal Elite was up and running. I had ten agents with varying skill levels, and I had every single one of them because Sebastian and Roone had bent over backward to accommodate me.

Any Royal Guard who left the service for some kind of family reason, or going to school, or anything like that, they funneled them my way. Any other security teams they'd worked with on travel missions that proved highly effective, again, they funneled my way. Two I had found on my own. So that felt like a good accomplishment.

But I'd been responsible for retraining everyone. I'd set the criteria, the business model, and I already had more business than I knew what to do with. Six months in, I was on my way to survival.

How had that even happened?

Well, it happened because of my family. I was going to have to get Sebastian some kind of insane present, or I could call Penny and just have her blow him on my behalf.

That was too weird. I owed them big though. And all I wanted to do was make them proud.

The phone on the bedside table buzzed. I ignored it. I didn't have anyone in the field at the moment, and I was tired. All I wanted to do was read my book. When I saw the screen said blocked number, I certainly wasn't going to answer it. Besides, no one in the islands had a blocked number from me, not with the encryption codes that Neela and I worked together to build.

I sat up and stared at the continually ringing phone.

Blocked number. *Bzzzt*.

Blocked number. *Bzzzt.*

My heart rate spiked with the hammering of my pulse. They rattled in my brain. Who could be calling so insistently?

How could it be so important that some unknown person would be calling me at eleven o'clock at night?

Finally, I gave in to the feelings of dread and picked up the phone. "This is Ariel."

There was silence. Even though all I heard was breathing on the other end, I knew who it was. Intrinsically, I knew. It was him.

I held onto my phone so tight, I was sure I was going to lose circulation in my fingers. The stupid tears pricked the backs of my lids and I fought for control. I was lying to Penny when I said I was getting over it.

I wasn't over shit. Just hearing him breathe evoked memories I wished were long dead. Memories that tore at the center of my chest, threatening to break me apart. Memories that were sweet and bitter and painful and beautiful. Memories I couldn't exorcise.

Memories I didn't *want* to exorcise.

And then he spoke.

It was only one word.

But it was a word spoken with a man's tone, not a boy's. It was a word spoken with a mixture of reverence and pain, worry and sadness. "Ariel..."

The tear escaped before I could stop it, rolling down my cheek. Why now? I was finally back to my life. Back where I needed to be.

But of course, my past was never going to let me go. "Your Highness."

"I—I'm sorry."

I blinked. He was sorry? For what? Was this the apology I'd been waiting for half my life? It took me a second to realize his words had been slurred.

He was drunk. He had to be. "Your Highness, perhaps—"

"I know. I shouldn't call. But I had to. Just to hear... your voice. Just one more time..."

What? One more time? "Tristan, what in the—" But I didn't get to finish... he'd already hung up.

To be continued in Return of the Prince...

THANK YOU

Thank you for reading TEMPTING THE HEIRESS! I hope you enjoyed this installment from the Royals Elite Series.

Curious about the mysterious Prince Tristan and the sassy determined Ariel? Find out what happens in the next book...Return of the Prince

They said I'd **never come home again**...**they were wrong.**

There is one person **worth returning home for**. *Her*. One little problem. **She hates me.**

She should, **I left her behind**.

Now I'm back and I have a **score to settle.**

I'll do what ever it takes to to **win her back.**

Even if it means spilling my secrets.

Pre-Order RETURN OF THE PRINCE Now>

Sign up for my newsletter to get new release alerts, exclusive bonus scenes and more: http://nanamaloneromance.net/newsletterlanding

NANA MALONE READING LIST

Looking for a few Good Books? Look no Further

FREE

Sexy in Stilettos

Game Set Match

Bryce

Shameless

Before Sin

Royals

Royals Undercover

Cheeky Royal

Cheeky King

Royals Undone

Royal Bastard

Bastard Prince

Royals United

Royal Tease

Teasing the Princess

Royal Elite

The Heiress Duet

Protecting the Heiress

Tempting the Heiress

The Prince Duet

Return of the Prince

To Love a Prince

The Bodyguard Duet

Billionaire to the Bodyguard

The Donovans Series

Come Home Again (Nate & Delilah)

Love Reality (Ryan & Mia)

Race For Love (Derek & Kisima)

Love in Plain Sight (Dylan and Serafina)

Eye of the Beholder – (Logan & Jezzie)

Love Struck (Zephyr & Malia)

London Billionaires Standalones

Mr. Trouble (Jarred & Kinsley)

Mr. Big (Zach & Emma)

Mr. Dirty(Nathan & Sophie)

The Shameless World

Shameless

Shameless
Shameful
Unashamed

Force
Enforce

Deep
Deeper

Before Sin
Sin
Sinful

Brazen
Still Brazen

The Player

Bryce
Dax
Echo
Fox
Ransom
Gage

The In Stilettos Series

Sexy in Stilettos (Alec & Jaya)

Sultry in Stilettos (Beckett & Ricca)

Sassy in Stilettos (Caleb & Micha)

Strollers & Stilettos (Alec & Jaya & Alexa)

Seductive in Stilettos (Shane & Tristia)

Stunning in Stilettos (Bryan & Kyra)

~~~

In Stilettos Spin off

Tempting in Stilettos (Serena & Tyson)

Teasing in Stilettos (Cara & Tate)

Tantalizing in Stilettos (Jaggar & Griffin)

The Chase Brothers Series

London Bound (Alexi & Abbie)

London Calling (Xander & Imani)

Love Match Series

**Game Set Match (Jason & Izzy)*

Mismatch (Eli & Jessica)

Don't want to miss a single release? Click here!
~~~

ABOUT NANA MALONE

USA Today Best Seller, Nana Malone's love of all things romance and adventure started with a tattered romantic suspense she "borrowed" from her cousin.

It was a sultry summer afternoon in Ghana, and Nana was a precocious thirteen. She's been in love with kick butt heroines ever since. With her overactive imagination, and channeling her inner Buffy, it was only a matter a time before she started creating her own characters.

Now she writes about sexy royals and smokin' hot bodyguards when she's not hiding her tiara from Kidlet, chasing a puppy who refuses to shake without a treat, or begging her husband to listen to her latest hair-brained idea.

Made in the USA
Columbia, SC
30 May 2020

98744887R00126